# MURDER IS NOT
# AN ODD JOB

**Also by Ralph Dennis**

*The War Heist*

**The Hardman Series**

*Atlanta Deathwatch*
*The Charleston Knife is Back in Town*
*The Golden Girl And All*
*Pimp For The Dead*
*Down Among The Jocks*
*Murder Is Not An Odd Job*
*Working For The Man*
*The Deadly Cotton Heart*
*The One Dollar Rip-Off*
*Hump's First Case*
*The Last Of The Armageddon Wars*
*The Buy Back Blues*

# MURDER IS NOT AN ODD JOB

RALPH DENNIS

BRASH
BOOKS

ISBN: 1-7324226-6-7
ISBN-13: 978-1-7324226-6-7

Published by Brash Books, LLC
12120 State Line #253,
Leawood, Kansas 66209
www.brash-books.com

# PUBLISHER'S NOTE

This book was originally published in 1974 and reflects the cultural and sexual attitudes, language, and politics of the period.

# CHAPTER ONE

It wasn't our kind of place. Not that Hump and I are snobs. Far from it. But this one belonged to the winos and their drinking doesn't have a red hair's worth of fun in it. It's all business: get as much as you can and then get it down before somebody comes over and asks for part of it. That kind of place, with the bare bones of survival sticking out, the smells and sounds of it.

Hump and I had been doing part of town, the underside of Atlanta. The last stop had been at the Fairmont, an old hotel that looks as if it might have been a movie theatre once. There's a lounge in back. To get to it, you've got to cross a parking lot that looks as if it might have been designed by a team of muggers. Nobody had bothered us and we spent about an hour there. There were three topless dancers and we stayed as long as we did because we got interested in the games they were playing.

It was after midnight when we left the lounge and went looking for a place to eat. Hump shook his head at the Majestic and we'd gone past that and turned onto Highland. I was thinking about some corned beef and that meant George's Deli, a place down near Virginia and Highland. We didn't get there. Hump was reading window signs. One stopped him: "PARKLAND DELI" and below that the neon flutter of "SANDWICHES and BEER." And that was how we ended up in wino haven.

It fooled us at first. The deli counter looked real enough and it wasn't until we moved past it, down a bottleneck aisle, that we realized what we'd stepped into. Narrow booths lined the walls and the faces that stared up at us had the bottle ruin on them. I

1

would have left but the bartender reached us and Hump ordered two Buds. We got the bottles of beer and looked at the glasses that came with them. The glasses didn't look clean and we drank out of the bottles.

"Why?" I asked.

Hump grinned at me. "Had this thirst."

To my left at the bar there was another man. After a couple of swallows of beer I got out my smokes and lit one. The man on my left turned and looked at the pack and I didn't wait for him to ask. I shook out three or four and held out the pack toward him. He settled for one and lit it with my matches.

"Appreciate it." His voice had a sandpaper rasp. It didn't seem to pain him any. It could have been an old injury or too many smokes. His age was hard to fix. He looked about fifty, about five-ten, with black hair and a flushed face. The bulb of his nose had a grain like pumice rock. "I haven't seen you two in here before."

It was early fall and he was wearing a red wool plaid shirt, tail out, over a tie shirt whose collar needed turning, tan pants, and heavy work shoes. And he was clean and shaved and his clothes had the smell of a laundry about them and that wasn't standard for the other men in the bar.

"It's our first time," I said. I pushed the heavy ash tray toward him. It was one of those two-pound glass ones that probably last forever. I guess that's why some bars buy them.

"It's not as bad as it looks," the man said.

Hump reached in behind me and touched me in the ribs. I eased the bar stool around and saw the man in the aisle, coming past the deli counter. He didn't belong in the place either. There was hood and badass stamped all over him. He was a tall, lank man in a belted trenchcoat, with a face as hard as an axe handle, and hands deep in his coat pockets.

"Know him?" Hump asked.

I shook my head. Nothing. And we weren't doing any job so he probably wasn't interested in us. He might have wandered into the wrong bar the same way we did. I put my back to him and faced the man in the red plaid shirt.

He said, "It's not the way you always hear it. These men aren't down on their luck. That's what they'll tell you. The truth is that they've given up on themselves."

"You a social worker?"

He laughed. It was a good laugh. "I'm one of them, I guess."

That seemed honest enough. I was about to follow up on that when two things happened. A big fat stud came in through the back door, from the parking lot or alley back there. He was carrying a pint of King Cotton in one hand. He stood in the doorway for a few seconds, swaying there, and looked around. I could have sworn he ran his eyes over us at the bar and then he shoved the pint bottle in his hip pocket and lumbered over to a wino standing near the bathroom door. He reached out a big hand and grabbed the wino by the shoulder.

"You stole a dollar off me," he said.

The wino said, "I don't even know you." He turned and tried to shake the fat man's hand off his shoulder.

The fat man said, "Son of a bitch!" and hit the wino with a fist that didn't have any fat on it. The fist hit the wino about throat high and put him down.

The bartender who'd waited on us came down the bar at a trot. He yelled, "Hey, stop that!" and he was clawing at a blackjack in his hip pocket. The pants were too tight and he was having trouble. But by the time the bartender reached the back of the bar he'd worked the blackjack free. He swung it back, ready to use it, but the fat man faked with a fist and kicked him in the balls. The bartender screamed and went down behind a table.

The place was emptying out. It was a stampede toward the back door. That would have been enough to hold my attention if I hadn't, for some reason, remembered the stud in the trenchcoat. I looked around, fully expecting that he'd left as soon as the fight broke out. He hadn't. He'd moved closer to the bar, now about even with Hump. He wasn't looking at Hump or me, but past me. That meant the guy in the plaid shirt on my left. Or someone in the back of the bar. About the time he was level with me, I heard the click and looked down at his right hand. I saw the flash of the blade when it jumped out of the cup of his hand.

Not my business, I thought. But I did a quick look at the junk on the bar. No club available. And then I remembered a trick from a bar in Oklahoma City. A waitress had used it on a drunken, horny cowboy that night. I caught the big ash tray in my right hand, spreading my fingers over the edges to grip it tight. Then I swung it around and hit the stud in the trenchcoat with a handball shot. But I'd been too slow. I heard a gasp from the man in the plaid shirt and I watched him grab at his back, fingers pressing his ribs on his right side. His eyes found me first, like he thought I'd used the blade on him. The anger was there just for a second because he saw the ash tray in my hand and the stud in the trenchcoat down on the floor.

One thing you could say for Hump. He didn't wait for explanations. As soon as he saw me clobber the guy, as soon as he saw the knife, he eased his stool around, planted one foot solidly on the floor, and kicked the trenchcoat man in the face a couple of times. The knife shook free and clattered over toward me. I leaned down and picked it up.

"Still thirsty?"

"I've had enough," Hump said.

I touched the man in the plaid shirt on the shoulder. "We can drop you at the hospital." I found the catch and closed the knife and shoved it in my pocket.

He shook his head. "It's not much."

I raised an eyebrow at Hump. He shrugged.

"Then we'll lend you a Bandaid instead."

I caught one of his arms and Hump caught the other and we went out the front door. Just before we went out, I looked back.

The fight was over and the fat guy had disappeared. The stud in the trenchcoat was still stretched out on the floor.

✤ ✤ ✤

It wasn't a bad cut. It was bleeding a little and it might have healed better with a couple of stitches. I washed the cut and spread on some first aid cream. I pulled the edges of the cut together and put on a couple of Bandaids side by side because I didn't have a bandage big enough to cover the wound.

When I was done, he went into the bathroom to wash up and I went into the kitchen. Hump had rummaged around and found the good bottle on the shelf behind the corn flakes. It was a cognac I was saving for later when the cold weather came. By the time I saw him, he'd worked the cork out and there wasn't much I could do but get down three glasses. Hump poured in three heavy shots.

He came in while we were sipping ours. He looked pale and a bit shaky. I pushed a glass of cognac toward him. "I don't think we know your name."

He hesitated for a long count of five, like he didn't know it either. Then, in the raspy voice, he said, "Ed Temple."

I told him I was Jim Hardman and the black dude gulping my twenty-five dollar cognac was Hump Evans.

"Twenty-five? This rotten hogwash?" Hump said.

Temple rolled a swallow of it around on his tongue and nodded at me. "Worth every penny of it."

"Speaking of pennies," I said.

"Yes?" There was a puzzled look on Temple's face.

"You been messing with loan sharks?"

"No."

"Owe a book?"

"I don't gamble."

"That's odd," I said, "because somebody wanted your gizzard chopped."

"That … back at the bar?"

I nodded.

"That wasn't meant for me," Temple said.

"You really believe that?"

Temple dipped his head. "This is the real grape you've got here." He held the glass in both hands, warming it, and pressed his nose down over the rim. After a few sniffs he must have realized I was still expecting more out of him. "I thought he was trying to cut you," he said.

"And you just happened to get in the way?"

"Yes."

Across the table from me Hump lowered his glass. "Might be."

I didn't believe it. I closed my eyes and ran it back like an instant replay. No chance. The stud in the trenchcoat had passed Hump and if he'd wanted me he wouldn't have been level with me. "Nope. He was passing me."

"See if Art knows him."

I used the phone in the bedroom. I got the Department and asked for Art Maloney in Homicide. We'd been good friends back in the old days, when I was on the force. But then I'd had to leave, about one step ahead of the boot, and he'd stayed on. Now, when I needed it, he was my plug into the Department. And I think we were still friends.

I ran the scene in the Parkland Deli by once for him.

"I'll ask around," Art said. "I can't make him."

"Call me."

"The one who was cut, what happened to him?"

"He's having a drink with us."

"And you think the cut was meant for him?"

"He says not."

"Bad cut?" he asked.

"Just broke the top skin."

"I'll get back to you."

Back in the kitchen, the clock Marcy had given me a couple of years back put the time at one-fifty. At the table, Hump tipped the bottle and ran each of us a good half shot.

"No help," I said.

"This is the nightcap." Hump slugged his back. "When is Marcy due back?"

I had to think it out. It was after midnight so it was Wednesday. "Sunday," I said.

"Where?"

"Frisco." It was some kind of convention for social workers. She'd left on Monday, a couple of days early, so she could spend those days in L.A. with an aunt before heading for Frisco and the meeting.

Hump stood up. "See you tomorrow?"

It was like that. Nothing much to do, and we hadn't had any kind of job for the last week or two, not even a shady one. So we'd have supper together and then some beers and the next thing I knew it was midnight. "Sure. Call me."

"A lift back to town?" Hump asked Ed Temple.

He hesitated and I figured he had the usual wino problem: no place to stay. I said, "You can have the sofa and I'll drop you in town in the morning."

He agreed to that. Hump left and I opened the sofa and tossed him a couple of clean sheets and a pillow and a blanket. "The place is yours." I undressed and got into bed. I was asleep about a minute after my head hit the pillow.

The pillow was on top. Under that the sheets and the blanket were neatly folded. Back in the kitchen he'd made himself a cup of instant coffee and he'd used the cup to anchor the note.

Thanks. I owe you one.
Ed Temple

It was ten-thirty. The saucepan, still with some water in it, was cold. So he'd left some time ago. So much for that. I put the cup in the sink, balled up the note and tossed it in the trash, and poured out the water from the saucepan and put in fresh. I got the paper and read the sports page while the water heated. I was on a second cup of coffee when Art called.

"Not sure about this. One guy I talked to says the man with the blade might be a stud from down in Tampa. Don't know his real name. He's called Ben Flash. Not the best in the world but not the worst either. Good enough to kill anybody but a pro." Art paused. "You got anybody mad at you, Jim?"

"Not that I know of,"

"The one who got cut..."

"He had my sofa last night. Took off before I got up."

"You think of a reason?"

"Probably needed a drink."

"Your shelf dry?"

"Maybe he didn't like my brands."

I had a couple of eggs and some sausage and some more coffee. It was about noon before I worked my way into the bathroom and started the shaky-handed shaving. I'd got about halfway down one cheek when I felt my toes kick something down around the side of the toilet. I leaned down and picked up a wallet. Ed Temple's, probably. I put it on the top of the water tank and finished my shave. I had a long hot shower and I was putting on aftershave when I saw the wallet again.

I carried it into the bedroom and tossed it on the bed. I finished dressing and then I picked it up and opened it. Good leather. Spanish goat. In the cash section I saw a twenty, a ten, and some ones, in the card section a handful of credit cards. I shoved the cards back in before I realized the cards were in the wrong name. He'd said Ed Temple and these cards were made out to Edward Templeton. Well, that was close. But a wino with a fistful of credit cards? That didn't make much sense.

Later in the afternoon I found myself on Marietta near the *Journal-Constitution* building. I went in and found the want ad counter and placed one in the personals.

> Edward Templeton. Have your wallet.
> Call me.

I added my phone number. I paid for the ad to run five days and then I met Hump and we had some drinks and I forgot about it. The forgetting was helped along by a couple of girls we met at Ruby Red's down in Underground Atlanta. Both of them seemed interested in Hump but I worked hard and ended up charming the ugly one.

# CHAPTER TWO

The black Continental parked on the road in front of my house just didn't belong there. It belonged a lot of other places: out West Paces, Ferry Road, or in some parts of Ansley Park. There it wouldn't look like a beautiful wart on a whore's nose.

I parked in the driveway and walked over into the center of my yard and looked at the Continental. I was hungover and screwed-out and tired and all I wanted was a hot shower and a day in bed. The ugly girl hadn't really been ugly after all and she'd been nice enough to say that I wasn't fat. It was a matter of posture and tightening up my stomach muscles. She'd shown me a few exercises before I thought of a couple I liked better. And I'd stayed longer than I'd intended to. Now it was Thursday morning and that damned Continental didn't seem to want to admit that I was looking at it.

The door on the far side of the Continental, the driver's side, opened and a big black stud in a gray chauffeur's uniform stepped out and came around the front of the car. He was carrying what seemed to be a newspaper with the subway fold creased into it. He moved like he hadn't spent much of his life on his ass. I noticed the rolling shoulders and the slim hips, and when he got closer, I saw that one nostril seemed to have continued to grow after the other had stopped: a boxer's disease, the result of a butt or a few solid rights.

About a step away from me he held out the paper. "You Jim Hardman?"

"Yeah."

"You place this ad?"

I took the paper from him and looked at the couple of lines that had been blocked out by four slashes of a blue felt-tipped pen. "That's mine." I flipped the paper back to him. "Why?"

"Mr. Foster wants to talk to you."

"Who?"

He didn't bother to answer. He opened the passenger door nearest us. The man who stepped out was Yale and J. Press and everything that went with that. He was about six feet tall, athletic in a handball or squash way, with gray hair and a neat gray mustache. His skin was tanned and it might have been Florida or the club sunlamp. Whatever else he might be, there was the mark of the dollar on him.

He crossed the lawn toward me as if he weren't really sure he ought to be doing this. It was a bit beneath him. But he'd started it and he was damned well going to finish it even if he had a heart attack. About two steps away he said, "I'm Arthur Foster of Foster, Mayberry, and Austin."

I took his hand and nodded. He already knew my name and I didn't see any reason to repeat it.

"I'd like a few words with you if you have the time."

I waved an arm at my house. "Come on in."

He followed me into the house with the chauffeur about a step behind him. Both of them looked around my living room as if they wished they'd brought gloves and protective clothing.

"Have a seat." I left them and got the tube of Alka Seltzer from the bathroom. Passing through the living room again on my way to the kitchen, I saw that Foster was seated on about three inches of the front edge of the sofa. The black chauffeur stood near the front door. In the kitchen I got down a glass and added a couple of inches of water and an ice cube. I carried the glass into the living room and they watched while I dropped in a couple of Alka Seltzer tablets. The ice cube would slow down the action of the tablets but it would be ice cold when I drank it.

"You told Roger you placed this ad." Foster said.

"That's right."

"I'd like to know the circumstances under which you came into possession of Edward Templeton's wallet."

"I'm not quite sure why you think you have a right to know."

At the door, Roger shifted his feet. I looked over at him. Foster didn't and I think that kept Roger nailed to the floor. Foster shook his head slightly. "Perhaps I should have explained. My law firm represents the Templeton business interests."

Business interests? That didn't sound like the wino Hump and I patched up during the early hours Wednesday. I lifted the glass and drank some of the fizz. The two tablets still hadn't dissolved. "I need to make a call. If you check out, I'll talk to you."

Foster nodded.

I went into the bedroom. Seated on the bed I could turn and look at him. I dialed the law office of Arnold Francher and got past his receptionist. I kept the small talk down. "You know a firm named Foster, Mayberry...and whatever?"

"Austin," Arnold said. "It's top drawer."

"Honest?"

"It has a good reputation."

"What does Foster look like?"

It matched all the way. It was Foster all right, or a damned good double.

"If this Foster told you he represented somebody, would you believe him?"

"One hundred percent."

"I owe you a drink," I said.

"And the full story."

I said goodbye and hung up. I went to the closet and got down the shoebox that holds my salted-away cash. It also holds my .38 Police Positive. I took out the .38 and stuck it down in my waistband and pulled my coat over it. Maybe it was unnecessary.

At the same time I'd felt the threat from the black chauffeur and I didn't like that. Not in my own living room.

Before I sat down across from Foster, I tossed back the Alka Seltzer. At the same time I let the coat fall open so they could see the butt of the gun. Sure it had registered with them, I sat down in the easy chair and waited.

"I trust I checked out."

"Arnold Francher talks about you as if you're God."

"I didn't know we had mutual friends."

I said, "I didn't know Arnold ran in high circles."

He brushed that aside. "Now, would you please tell me about the wallet?"

I did. The whole story, from the time we walked into wino haven until I put Edward Temple or Templeton to bed on my sofa. I watched him when I talked about the knife man. He didn't flinch. I guess that's something lawyers learn in court.

At the end he said, "I was afraid of that."

"Afraid of what?"

"That something like this might happen."

"That somebody might try to off him?" I said.

"Off?"

"Kill."

"Perhaps." He drew back the cuff on his right wrist and looked at his watch. "It is ten-fifteen now. Are you free at one-thirty this afternoon?"

"I might be. Why?"

"Some people would like to talk to you."

"About what?"

"I'd rather not tell you what they're going to say. It might spoil their considerable pleasure."

"Why me?"

"I've done some checking on you."

"And you're going to tell me you like what you've heard?"

"Not exactly." The smile could have had a sneer buried in it but it didn't. "But let me say that I've been in law long enough to develop some understanding."

That was fair enough. He knew about my time with the Department and the way I'd left it. And if he'd talked to the right people, he knew about the kinds of jobs Hump and I did to make a living. "Who'd you talk to?"

"Rex Martin."

I nodded. Rex was in Homicide and he probably didn't like me but I'd helped him out a time or two.

"And he passed me on to a Mr. Art Maloney."

"He could have told you about the wallet," I said.

"He did," Foster said, "but I wanted to hear your version of it." He stood up. "This is a fairly complicated matter and I'd rather you heard about it in the presence of the family."

"What family?"

"The Templeton family." He moved around the coffee table and stopped next to the chauffeur, Roger. "If you agree to come, Roger will pick you up at exactly ten after one. It is a twenty-minute drive from here to the Towers."

"All right."

"And you won't need the pistol."

I grinned at him. "I wasn't sure I needed it here. But your man looks like he might be a hard ass."

Roger grinned at me. "I know your friend, Mr. Evans."

"Well, Atlanta's a small town and Hump's no midget."

"About two hundred and seventy, the last time I guessed his weight," Roger said.

"What's your last name?"

"Brown," he said, "but you might know of me as Eddie Jacks."

He was right. I did. He'd been a good light heavy back in the late sixties. He'd been getting close to the top ten in his class when some dumb pug ducked and Roger had shattered some bones in his left hand on the pug's head. That pug must have had a head like a steel door. The bones hadn't healed well. "I wondered what happened to you."

"Now you know."

Foster stepped between us. "You'll be ready at ten after one?"

I dropped an eyelid at Roger. "I might just come along so Roger can tell me about life in the fight game."

"It's no life," Roger said.

I saw them out and then I set my clock for twelve-thirty. I went to bed and I could feel the ugly girl's fingerprints all over me before I dropped over the edge.

⚜ ⚜ ⚜

Our destination was the Melton Towers far out Peachtree Road. Roger drove into the curving drive out front and stopped. He said the Templetons were on the twelfth floor. I'd have to tell the security men at the door that I was expected.

"What apartment?"

Roger grinned at me. "The whole floor."

"You leaving?"

"The interview with you is from one-thirty to two. I'll be out front waiting when you come out."

"What if I don't last the whole half hour?"

"You will."

There were two security men at the front door. They checked my name in a log and then they ran through my whole card file of identification. Then one of the security men escorted me to the elevator and rode up to the twelfth floor with me. After we stepped out into a foyer with a desk and another security man seated behind it, he remained with me until Foster came from the apartments beyond and nodded at him.

"What is this," I asked Foster, "the local branch of Fort Knox?"

"Not exactly."

We passed through the foyer and into a wide, large living room. It was a room that didn't look lived in. It had about as much personality as an airport toilet bowl. The sofa, the chairs, the tables looked untouched by human hands or rumps.

"This way," Foster said.

He was gesturing toward an entranceway off to the right. I kept him waiting while I sat down in one of the straight-backed chairs. There. Now one rump had touched one of the chairs.

It was a hospital bed and it could have been a hospital room. But it wasn't painted white and the two paintings I recognized were a Matisse and a Cezanne. The two others I didn't recognize were probably equally expensive but I hadn't had time for Art Appreciation I at Georgia State.

The man in the bed was about a breath and a half away from death. The half breath would be the one he died on. He'd probably never been a large man. Now the flesh had wasted away from him, as if he'd melted and been left with nothing but bones. With the flesh gone from his face, his teeth looked large and out of proportion.

He used one breath looking at me and then Foster stepped close to the bed and said, "This is Mr. Hardman, the gentleman I told you about." At the same time Foster motioned me closer, until my knees were against the iron frame of the bed.

"He … doesn't … look … like a gentleman … to me."

"I'm not," I said. "That's just the way lawyers talk."

I could have sworn he laughed then. When it came out it sounded like air hissing out of a punctured tire tube.

"I ... don't ... think Foster ... approves ... of you."

"Not many people do," I said. "Even my girlfriend has that kind of day now and then."

The man in the bed looked at me for about a count of five. A hand with the blue veins showing across the back crabbed its way down the sheet and stopped. There wasn't anything for it to touch and I guess it gave up. "Hire ... him," he said.

He closed his eyes. The interview was over. Foster and I went out. Out in the small living room that went with this apartment we passed a nurse who could have played right guard, or even left, on the Falcons.

"Who was that?"

"I don't know her name," Foster said.

"I meant the man in the bed."

"I thought you knew."

I shook my head.

"That was Rufus Templeton." The way he said it implied I ought to know the name.

"I don't even read the stock market pages," I said.

"Steel, oil, even a big block of Coca-Cola at one time."

"Worth how much?"

He shook his head. "The figures would impress you but they wouldn't mean that much to you. Let me say only that it is a sizable holding." He looked at me with amazement. "You knew Eddie Jacks but you've never heard of Rufus Templeton."

"Every man to his own sport." I looked at my watch. The interview hadn't taken the whole half hour. "Is that all?"

"Mrs. Fanzia wants to meet you."

"Who's she?"

"Mr. Templeton's daughter."

"Which one?"

"Rufus Templeton. She is also Edward's sister."

"I see."

"I hope all this isn't confusing you," Foster said.

"I'll get the scorecard straight sooner or later."

We moved into another part of the floor. It was subtle at first and then it got stronger. The decor was changing and becoming more and more feminine, as if we'd left one home and gone to another one. And then we turned a corner and we were in a small sitting room. It was something out of a play or an old English movie. I had the feeling that Elizabeth Barrett Browning or one of the Brontes would step out any second and start talking about the latest poem or novel they'd written.

"Real?" I asked, looking at the furniture.

"Absolutely," he said.

Then the woman stood up and walked toward us. I'd seen the type before but never close enough to touch. She had dark hair and skin that would have pleased a girl twenty years old, a thin white dress that missed her knees by about four inches, and slim legs and thighs that could squeeze the life out of a man or put life back into him.

All of that and the woman was somewhere between forty and fifty.

"Mr. James Hardman," Foster said, introducing us.

The hand that touched mine was soft and appeared to give off a feeling of warm oil. And a smell too. The smell of flesh wanting to give up and grow old while the woman's will wouldn't let it.

"Is it too early for a drink?" she asked.

"I think not." As soon as I said it, I realized that I'd fallen into talking like somebody out of that English play or movie.

"Scotch for me," she said to Foster.

I nodded. "And a rock." I said that just to shake the English out of my head. And I promised myself I'd say "crap" or "shit" the first chance I got.

"Do you mind, Arthur?" she said to Foster.

"Of course not."

I wanted to watch him mix the drinks. I couldn't. I kept coming back to her. There must be at least one woman like her in the dream, the fantasy life of most men. I'd been luckier than most. I'd ended up in bed with mine and it made me skeptical about make-up and foundation garments. As I remember, when she took off her girdle the fat ran down her legs like ice cream down the side of a cone.

"You were a policeman, I believe," she said.

"For a time, Mrs. Fanzia."

"Please call me Beth."

I nodded. Foster finished at the sideboard and brought us our drinks. I noticed he hadn't made one for himself. I took a sip of mine and found that it was the pure dew. Glenlivet, I guessed.

Beth sipped her drink. "I must admit it was rather an odd story you told Foster here."

"But true." I reached into my jacket pocket and brought out the blade I'd picked up from the floor that night. I did the flip and the blade jumped out at her.

"It looks like a knife anyone could buy at a pawn shop."

"Except that this one is somebody's old friend." I passed the knife to her. "Notice the width of the blade."

"It's awfully thin."

"Either it's been cut down on purpose or over a period of years it's been used and honed and used and honed until it's lost about twenty percent of the blade surface."

She returned the knife to me and I closed the blade and dropped it in my pocket.

Foster said, "Why would a knife be cut down on purpose?"

"It's the difference between a cutter and a stabber. I think our man was a stabber. He'd walk up to somebody like your brother—helped out by the fight in the back of the bar—and place the blade in him a time or two. No slashing, just in and out, and then he'd lean the dead man up against the bar and walk away."

"And nobody would notice?"

"In that kind of bar it might be half an hour before the bartender noticed him and shook him and told him to go home and sleep it off."

Beth shuddered. "Why would anyone want to hurt Edward?"

"I don't know that much about him. My first guess was loan sharking but he said he wasn't into that. Beyond that, your guess is as good as mine.

"How much has Foster told you?"

"Nothing." I took another sip of the single malt. "I've had the tour and your father has looked me over and he said something about hiring me. Now I'm here and I still don't know what this is all about."

Beth got a cigarette from a silver box on the table next to her. Foster had his lighter out and flaming before I could get mine out of my pocket. "My father is going to die soon."

"It looks that way," I said.

"There's quite a bit of money involved and my brother Edward is going to inherit it."

"If...," Foster said.

"If he lives until after the death of Daddy."

"If he doesn't," I said, "who's next in line?"

"I am." Beth blew a slow curl of smoke at me.

"I'm confused." I stood up and to cover the confusion I went over to the sideboard and tipped a slug of Glenlivet into my glass and added another ice cube from the silver bucket. "What is it exactly that you people want to hire me for?"

"I want you to keep Edward alive."

"Why?" I came back to my chair and stood there, looking down at her.

"That's a strange question," Foster said. There was a snort of the insulted in his tone.

"It might be." I didn't look at him. I wanted to read whatever there was to see on Beth's face. "It's also an honest question. As far as I can tell, Beth, you have the most to gain from Edward's death."

"It's not that simple. You see, I love my brother very much, more than any amount of money. Oh, it would be nice to have all that money. It would be an absolute rip. Still, one of the nicest things about Edward is that he has no interest at all in money."

"The will makes more than adequate provision for Mrs. Fanzia," Foster said.

"Who then?"

Foster looked puzzled.

"Who wants Edward Templeton dead?"

"I don't know."

I shrugged and came around the chair and sat down. Across from me Beth crossed her legs at the knees. I could see the edge of her underpants. No girdle. And there wasn't a spare ounce of flesh on the back of her thighs. So much for the woman with the fat running down her legs like ice cream.

"I'd like to see the will."

"That's not possible," Foster said.

"Then you're asking me to blunder around in the dark. The best way to keep Edward alive is to find out who wants to kill him and stop it at that end."

"I think I can outline it for you. The bulk of the estate, after the provisions for Mrs. Fanzia, goes to Edward. If Edward dies before his father, then Mrs. Fanzia is the heir." Foster spread his hands and looked at them. "It is really quite straightforward."

"And if both Edward and Beth die before Mr. Templeton?"

Foster blinked. I could see that I'd hit some sensitive place beyond the reserve. It was better than saying crap or shit. "In such a case, the estate would go to his grandson, his only grandson."

"My son, Rudolph," Beth said. "He is ten now."

"Where is he now?"

"With his father in Venice."

"Is his father still in Venice?"

"I suppose so," she said.

"I'd like to be sure."

Beth stubbed out her smoke in a crystal ash tray. "I don't understand."

"I think you do. People kill for a lot of reasons. Mainly they kill for love and money. There's enough money involved here so we can forget about love. It's money. Assuming you don't want Edward dead, I think we ought to concentrate on your husband…"

"My ex-husband," she said.

"Ex-husband, then."

"What do you want me to do?"

"I'd like for you to call your ex-husband. I'd like to be sure he's still in Venice."

She nodded.

"I'll call you later," I said.

"The number isn't listed."

Foster took a card from a small leather case and wrote on the back of it. He passed the card to me. "When will you call?"

I looked at Beth. She said, "I'll try to reach him in an hour or so. If you'll give me your number, Mr. Hardman, I'll call you as soon as I know anything."

"You can call me at Edward's place." I got out my pad. "I'll need his address."

I saw the blank look on her face but I didn't understand it.

"We should have told you, Mr. Hardman, we don't really know where Edward lives."

That tore some of it. Still it fitted with the rest of the kooky setup. "Then I guess the first business is to find him."

"Of course." She stood up and held out her hand again. I had to walk over a few steps to touch it. I had the funny feeling that I was supposed to kiss her on the knuckles.

"I might need to talk to you again," I said.

"Any time you need me," she said.

Foster walked out with me. At the doorway I looked over my shoulder at her. There was a faint tracing of a smile on her face. I guess I'd said the right thing to trigger her vanity. Without meaning to.

Foster rode the elevator down with me.

"We haven't talked about money."

"I knew we'd get around to it sooner or later," I said.

"I don't think there will be any problem."

"It's a hundred a day for me and a hundred a day for my buddy."

"This is the Evans that Roger mentioned?"

I nodded. "And expenses, of course. If it gets hairy, we might be moving around quite a bit. That would be pretty expensive."

We stepped out into the lobby. The two security guards turned and watched us as we walked toward the main doors. "I'll send you a check for a thousand dollars this afternoon."

"If it's all the same to you, I'd like it in cash. Twenties. If it gets hot, I won't have time to cash checks."

Foster understood that. "Call me in an hour and tell me where you want the money delivered. I'll have Roger bring it to you."

The Continental, with Roger holding the passenger door open, waited at the driveway curb.

# CHAPTER THREE

After we dropped Foster at Colony Square, the huge new development of office buildings and apartments that covers a block on Peachtree between 14th and 15th, I gave Roger Hump's address and we headed back downtown. At 11th Street we caught a red light and I got out and moved up front and sat next to Roger.

"I can't stand success." I said. Roger grinned at me. "And back there I'd expect people to throw rocks at me."

"Different strokes," he said and I knew he was talking about Foster.

The light changed and we headed through the Strip, once a hippie and street people hangout, now dying on the vine and turning to dust. "You know Edward Templeton?"

"Some," he said.

"How long?"

"About as long as anybody."

I got out my smokes and lit one and held the pack toward him. He shook his head. "How long is that?"

"A month. Since he showed up in Atlanta."

That bounced around in my head for a few seconds. It kept bouncing about a foot out of my reach. "I don't understand."

"I thought they'd tell you. Edward ain't been heard of for years and years and years until a month ago. I guess he heard his Daddy was sick and he came back to see him."

"How many years?"

"You'd have to ask them to be sure. The way I heard it, a lot of years."

"Where'd he been?"

"I didn't hear," he said.

I didn't see an ash tray so I found a button and got the window down and tapped some ashes out into the slipstream. "What do you think of him?"

"Straight?"

"Straight."

"He's a strange dude. Looks at you like he don't care if you're black or white or red or purple-striped. And there's something inside him, like he's at peace. Like he's been studying one of those Eastern religions." His eyes wrinkled at the corners. "Take you. This ain't putting the bad mouth on you. Hump runs with you and that's good enough for me. That is a grade A stamp. But you're always aware. I feel it. You know you're white and you're talking to a black and it's like you're always watching to see how your white is getting along with my black. Not that Edward dude. He just jumped past that somewhere."

"It's a good move if you can make it," I said. And because there was a lot of truth in it, I could feel the sweat start under my arms.

"It sure changes the ground rules," Roger said.

"He sounds like some kind of saint."

"He might be."

I got tired of the slipstream. I tossed out the butt and closed the window. "Who's trying to kill him?"

"Man, I don't know."

"But you know somebody is?"

"Heard you talking to Mr. Foster over at your place," he said.

"No guess before that?"

"Maybe one."

"Tell me about it."

"One day he was over at Mr. Foster's office and Mr. Foster told me to drive him wherever he wanted to go. Sat right where you are now. I noticed he kept rubbing his shoulder and I asked him about it. Lying just ain't in that man. He said a car almost hit him and he had to dive to get out of the street."

"When was that?"

"Two or three weeks ago."

That nailed it. Two attempts on his life that we knew about. The mechanical one hadn't worked, so they had gone to the blade and the hand-to-hand. "He say anything more about it?"

"That was it. To him it was just something that happened and he'd accepted it and forgot about it except for the shoulder."

I leaned back and closed my eyes.

"Hard night?"

"It show that much?"

"Like a birthmark," he said.

A few minutes later he dropped me in front of Hump's apartment.

Hump blinked at me through the partly opened door and said, "Shit, the next party don't start for another twelve hours."

"Business."

He swung the door open and stepped aside. By the time he'd finished with the shower, I had a couple of cups of coffee made. His cooled some while he dressed. He came in carrying his socks and shoes and sat down at the kitchen table. He sipped the coffee and put on his socks and shoes while he listened me out.

"Lord, I love those fairy tales," he said at the end of it.

"It's got that flavor."

"You mean that old wino is going to be worth millions?"

"If he lives that long," I said. "What do you think about the job?"

"It's better than pimping for a living."

That was a joke. So far Hump hadn't gone into that. He's six-six or seven and two-seventy and black and at one time he was one of the best defensive ends in pro football. He played for Cleveland, until he tore up a knee and lost a couple of steps. For the last few years he and I have been doing odd jobs for a living. Anything that stops short of killing. To Hump, pimping is a bit worse than killing.

Roger brought over a thick envelope of twenties an hour later. I answered the door and waved him inside. Hump looked out of the bathroom with shaving cream on his face and waved at Roger. I dropped the envelope on the kitchen table and asked him if he wanted a coffee.

"Why not?"

I heated up the water and made him a cup of instant. "One thing that got lost in the confusion," I said. "Nobody told me where Edward lives."

"I thought you knew."

"Knew what?"

"Nobody knows where he lives."

Oh, shit. That meant we'd really have to find him before we could start trying to keep him alive. "No guesses?"

"Just one. It might be over in that section near Ponce de Leon and Highland."

"Why?"

He sipped the coffee and made a face. "That's godawful coffee."

"So don't marry me." I waited. "Why?"

"One time he had me drop him at the bus stop. I had to circle the block. When I came back by, he was getting on a number 2 bus. It was the number 2 Ponce de Leon and Frederica bus that don't go past Highland. It's not like the Ponce de Leon and Decatur bus."

"Good eyes," I said.

"And another time, when he knew me better, he let me drop him at that bar, the one where you met him the other night."

"The Parkland Deli."

"That's the one."

"It's a place to start," I said.

When Hump was ready, we walked out together. Out on the street we stopped next to the Continental. "You got a phone where we can reach you?"

"I'm in the book. The Roger Brown on Boulevard."

"It gets rough, we might need a hand."

"I'm not a pro."

"It gets rough, it might not matter."

Roger looked past me, toward Hump. Hump said, "Jim's taught me everything I know about the business. It took him all of five minutes."

"Call me then. I kind of like that Edward dude."

It was the same bartender from a couple of nights before. It was still early but there were several tables of winos hunched over their beer glasses. When the bartender brought our Buds, I watched the way he walked. He was still ball-sore from the kick the fat man had put on him. Otherwise he didn't seem to be marked.

"Quite a brawl you had here the other night," I said.

"You here for that?"

"At the bar."

He stared at me for a long moment. "Yeah, I remember you now."

"You know the fat guy started it?"

"He's not a regular."

"And probably won't ever be," I said, grinning at him.

"Not if I see him first."

"Figured as much." I waited a beat or two and then, trying to keep it as casual as I could, I said, "When the fight broke out, I was talking to one guy here at the bar. A guy about forty-five or fifty, wearing a red plaid shirt. Had a hoarse voice. You know him?"

"Sure. Eddie comes around now and then."

"Every day?"

"Mostly."

I could feel the surge of distrust. I'd seen it in enough bars. Bars are homes for some people and all the skiptracers and bill collectors end up at the bars in time, looking for this guy or that one. And all bartenders have a way of protecting their regulars.

"You know where he lives?"

He shook his head.

"In the area?"

"I don't know."

"I'm not tracing or collecting," I said. "And it's important."

"I don't know him that well."

"Who would?" I swung around on my bar stool and looked at the tables of winos. "Any of those?"

"You straight with me?"

"It's important and I'm not after him for anything."

"I thought you were a cop," he said.

"Not anymore."

He nodded toward the last table, the one nearest the back entrance. "The skinny one in the red shirt. I've seen him talking to Eddie some. He might know, if he'll talk to you."

"What's his name?"

"They call him Rat."

"What are they drinking?"

"Pabst draft."

I got out a five and dropped it on the bar. "Draw me a big one."

Rat looked up at me when I stopped in the aisle next to the table. There were three of them at the wino social, Rat on one side of the table and two others facing him. Up close, Rat's eyes seemed to come within a red hair of matching the color of his shirt. On the center of the table there was a small pitcher with about a half inch of beer in it.

"You got room for this?"

The two I wasn't talking to, eager, pushed the almost empty pitcher aside to make room. Rat just looked at me. "Why you giving away beer?"

"I thought you might do me a favor."

I put the pitcher down and the other two filled their glasses. One lifted the pitcher and pointed the spout at Rat's glass but he put his hand over the rim and shook his head. "What kind of favor?"

"I need to get in touch with Eddie."

"I don't know any Eddie."

"You know him."

"Sure, you know Eddie, Rat," one of the others said. I looked at him. He was about forty, red glint of whiskers and a couple of dirt pimples on his nose.

"Maybe you could help me then," I said to the one who'd spoken.

"He don't know any Eddie either," Rat said.

"You know Eddie got cut the other night."

"I might know that," Rat said, "if I knew anybody named Eddie."

"I'm the one with the ash tray."

His eyes registered that. He knew about it.

"And I was the one put a couple of Bandaids on the cut."

Rat looked past me toward the bar where Hump was. "That the black guy who was with you?"

"That's him."

Rat lifted his hand from the top of his glass. The one with the dirt pimples poured him a shaky glass of beer. "What do you want with Eddie?"

"I need to talk to him."

"Maybe he don't want to talk to you."

"That might be, but you could ask him."

"I might."

"Call him," I said.

"No telephone."

"If it's far I'll pay the cab fare."

He lifted the beer glass and poured the whole glassful down in one steady stream. "It about the other night?"

I nodded.

He pushed back his chair. "I'll be back." He moved away from the table and then came back. "Don't follow me."

"And leave my beer?" I looked at him like he was crazy.

When Rat passed the bar, Hump turned on his stool and dropped his feet to the floor, ready to follow Rat. I shook my head at him and he turned and planted his elbows on the bar again. I returned to the bar and ordered two more Buds.

He came in quietly. I didn't know he'd arrived until the bartender leaned right past me and said, "You drinking, Eddie?"

"A draft," he said in that rasping voice of his.

I turned and looked at him. He was dressed about the same: gray work pants, a faded denim shirt, the red plaid shirt with the tail out and the heavy work shoes.

"Join us," I said. "How's the side?"

"Itches like the devil," he said.

"I heard somewhere that means it's healing."

Eddie paid for his draft. "Rat said you wanted to see me."

"You left your wallet at my place the other night."

"I wondered where it was."

"It's got money and credit cards in it."

"You looked in it?"

"Far enough to know the name's Templeton rather than Temple."

He stared at me, trying to read in my face whether Templeton meant anything to me. It was a trick I knew how to handle. I looked him right in the eyes and thought of boiled cabbage. When that didn't work anymore, I'd think of baked eggplant. Or chick-peas.

"Appreciate you bringing it down to me."

That was my cue to bring the wallet out, if we were what we seemed to be, nice guys going a little out of our way. So far I hadn't figured how to tell Edward we'd been hired to protect him until his father, the old man, died. I had a feeling that it wasn't an arrangement he was going to care much for.

I turned to Hump and lowered an eyelid at him. "Let me have the wallet, Hump."

"Huh? I haven't got it."

"You had it last. Right before we left my place."

"I thought you picked it up," Hump said.

Good man. He'd played it well without very much warning. I eased back around to face Edward. "A fuck-up of sorts."

"I heard." He tossed back the bottom third of his beer. "You can drop it by the next time you're in the area. Just leave it with the bartender and I'll get it."

"Better than that," I said, "why don't you ride out to my place with us? You can pick up your wallet and I can take another look at that cut."

"I don't know ..." He let it trail off.

"Some problem?"

"I don't know you two," he said evenly.

"There's not much to know. Big guy there is Hump Evans. Used to play pro ball."

"Hump's not your real name?"

"It's the one I answer to most of the time."

"And I'm Jim Hardman. Ex-cop."

The bartender came over and looked at Edward's empty glass. Edward shook his head. "This isn't a question I usually ask. Maybe you won't mind. What do you two do for a living?"

"As little as possible," I said.

"Odd jobs," Hump added.

"But not murder?"

I wanted him to believe me. "No. Murder is not an odd job. It's a profession."

He bought it. "I'll ride out with you."

While he was at the back table talking to Rat, I called the bartender over and paid for another large pitcher of draft, to be taken back after we'd left.

I made a wide loop on the way home. At the seafood market on Ponce de Leon I bought three pounds of shrimp. On down a few blocks I stopped at the Royal Bakery. I walked in among the huge high racks of cooling bread and picked out a loaf of French.

First thing after we arrived at my place, I gave him the wallet. While he looked at it, I went into the kitchen and started peeling the shrimp, leaving the tail on, and deveining them. I was trying out a new method. I used a new ejector razor blade and it worked pretty well after I got over the fear that I'd slice off a finger or two.

Hump and I switched to Scotch on the rocks. Edward settled for a beer. While I peeled and deveined, Hump got him to take off his shirt. Hump pressed a wet cloth to the Bandaids before he tried to take them off. It wasn't necessary. Edward had taken it easy in the last day or two. The edges of the cut were growing together well and a thready crust was forming.

Even with the ejector blade slicing along, three pounds of shrimp takes a bit of time. "You'll stay to supper, Edward?"

"Scampi *al burro?*" He'd seen me take out the garlic, the green onions, and the lemons.

"Good guess."

"It's been a long time."

"It's settled, then."

"There's one thing, though. I get a kind of feeling about you and Hump, that you're not being entirely honest with me."

"You read it right." I was getting down to the last third of the shrimp and I didn't want to stop. "I didn't know how to get in touch with you so I ran an ad in the paper. You didn't see it but the family lawyer, Foster, did."

"And?"

"I got the tour of the old home place and I met your father and I talked to your sister."

"I thought it might be something like that." He didn't sound angry or disappointed, just tired.

"You mind if I finish these shrimp before we talk about it?"

"No. I'll have another beer."

Hump got it for him and I started the downhill side with the last pound of shrimp.

"I've got to make a call. You can come with me."

He sat on the edge of the bed while I dialed the number Foster had written on the card for me. I had to work my way through two people before I got Beth Fanzia on the line.

"Yes, Mr. Hardman?"

"You make the overseas call?"

"An hour ago."

"And?"

"He is not in Venice. My son, Rudolph, is in the country with an aunt. I spoke to the housekeeper. She said the count is in Rome but she doesn't have a number where he can be reached."

"Is that usual?"

"You don't know my ex-husband's sexual appetites."

"Sorry." I looked over at Edward. He didn't even seem to be listening to my part of the conversation. "Did she say when he left for Rome?"

"Four days ago."

"Then he could be in this country?"

"I don't think he'd come without calling me," she said.

Like shit. Like cow shit and horse shit mixed together. "We can check it out. How's he listed in his passport?"

"Count Alfredo Fanzia."

"Thank you, Beth." I tapped Edward on the shoulder. "Edward's here with me. He's staying to supper. Would you like to talk to him?"

"Yes. But what should I say to him?"

"Whatever you want to. But I've got a feeling he'd rather not buy this deal I made with you and Foster."

"Let me speak to him."

I passed the receiver to Edward and went back into the kitchen. I melted the butter in a skillet and added a few drops of olive oil so the butter wouldn't burn. Then I browned a few cloves of garlic and the green onions, tops and all. While this worked off, I turned on the broiler and arranged the shrimp in a shallow baking pan. Right at the end I added lemon juice and salt and pepper.

Hump uncorked the bottle of Riesling I'd put out on the back steps to cool. "How's he taking it?"

"His sister's talking to him. If she doesn't carry the right weight, we might be out of a job. Or we'll have to watch him from a distance, against his will."

"That's the hard way."

"And the risky one," I said. I poured the butter sauce over the shrimp and ran them under the broiler. After a couple of minutes I checked them. The shrimp were turning and curling. I used a spoon to turn each shrimp and then I basted the shrimp once more before I put them back under the broiler.

Edward came back from the bedroom while I was giving them a final check. "Well?"

"Beth makes a good argument."

"But not good enough?"

"I can't go along with it."

I lifted out the pan of shrimp. "No way to change your mind?"

"Not unless you kidnap me."

"That's not an odd job either." The room filled with the scent of butter and garlic and onions. "Let's have supper anyway."

I portioned out the shrimp, about a pound to each of us, and poured the butter over them. We drank the wine and ate and used the still-warm French bread to sop up the sauce.

Hump stacked the dishes in the sink while Edward and I sat over coffee. I needed some new way to convince Edward to change his mind, but I couldn't come up with one. From all accounts there'd been two attempts on his life. If that didn't shake him, I couldn't think of anything that would.

"It's a mistake, Edward." I knew how lame that was.

"I've been a private person for a long time. It's too late to become someone else now."

"You've set yourself up. It'll be easier for whoever wants to kill you."

"I think I'm old enough to die," he said.

He wanted us to drop him at the Parkland Deli. We were half a block away when I saw the red flashing light on the top of a police car. It seemed to be parked in front of the beer joint. I drove past and turned onto St. Charles and parked. The three of us walked back to the Parkland. There were a number of uniformed cops and a couple of plainclothes men I recognized. One of them was Art Maloney. I told Hump and Edward to wait and I went over close enough to call to Art.

He broke away from the group. "What you want, Jim?"

"What happened? Another brawl?"

"Worse," he said. "A dead man out in the back parking lot."

"Who?"

"Some wino. Nobody knows his real name. They call him Rat."

"How?"

"Knifed. But that was later. Looks like somebody broke his arm and a few of his fingers."

"Put some questions to him?"

"Might be. Why are you interested?"

"I'll call you."

"No." He caught my arm. "Now."

I pulled my arm free. "I'll call you in an hour."

"You'd better."

I pushed through a crowd of watchers. Before I could explain what had happened, the men from the meat wagon pushed the front door open and wheeled out the stretcher bed. There was a covered body on it.

"You know who that is?" I asked Edward.

He shook his head.

"It's getting rough. That's your friend, Rat."

"Why? Why would …?"

I caught one arm and Hump caught the other one. He didn't protest as we walked him down Highland and around the corner to the car. Once we were inside, I lit a smoke and blew some of it out the window. I had to make the choice sooner than I'd planned to. And the parts were scattered and hard to bring together.

"It looks like kidnaping is all that's left."

I kicked the engine over and pulled across the street into the A & P lot to make my turn. We headed back down Highland past the Parkland Deli. When we were level with the meat wagon, one of the attendants slammed the back door shut. It seemed, for some reason, a gesture with a lot of finality to it.

# CHAPTER FOUR

I t might have been the first motel ever built in Georgia. At least it looked that way. Instead of the solid bank of rooms shoved together it was a series of small clapboard cabins yards and yards apart. Huge old pines towered over the cabins. The office might have been just another of the cabins except for the lighted sign above the door. "PINEVIEW MOTEL. REASONABLE RATES."

If the blonde woman in her forties was surprised that she had guests registering, she hid it well while I filled out the card. I put down a new name. Jim Harper. It was close enough so I'd answer to it. And a new address, 641 Bellevue Drive, Anderson, South Carolina. Why not? I'd never been to Anderson and I didn't know anyone else who had either.

She turned the card so she could read the name there. "How long will you be staying, Mr. Harper?"

"One night, I think."

I could see that she was peering out at the driveway. I'd parked out of the window sightlines. I'd put down the right make of the car but I'd transposed some when I'd written down the license plate numbers. I didn't think she'd notice but if she did, who knew their own phone number or license plate that well?

I paid for the first day in advance and got the key and the directions to unit six, and the information that there was a restaurant about half a mile down the road.

The cabin was larger inside than I'd thought. Two single beds, a couple of chairs and a battered black and white television set in the main room. In back there was a small bathroom with a shower stall. All the walls were real knotty pine.

Edward looked around and then sat down on the edge of one of the beds. "I don't think I understand this."

Hump came back from his check of the bathroom. He stood in the doorway and waited. I could see that he had his doubts too, but he hadn't said anything so far.

"Simple enough. Before they killed Rat, they probably asked him some questions." I said. "The big question they might have asked was where you were. Did you tell him?"

"I told him who you were and that I was going with you to pick up my wallet."

"Then it's better than even money they're fucking around my house right now."

"What happened to Rat?"

"You don't really want to know that."

I walked to the door. Hump followed me.

"I've got to run into town for an hour or so," I said. Hump raised an eyebrow at me. "To get some underwear for all of us, some sandwiches, and something to drink."

It wasn't the whole truth but it was close enough to satisfy Edward if he asked the same question.

It must have been the scare hour at pawnshops, the hour when all the robberies take place. The clerk behind the counter jumped at the sound of the bell on the door. I gave the bell another shake before I closed the door and walked over to him.

"Paul in?"

"Does he know you?"

"He knows me," I said.

He led me through a doorway and down a dark hallway to an office in the bowels of the building. Paul was at a table in the corner of the room, heating himself a can of soup on a one-burner hot plate. He looked at me and grinned and I said, "Tell your man here I'm not going to knock over the place."

"It's all right," Paul said. "And close the door after you, John."

Paul's a dapper man. He looks like my idea of what a headwaiter disguises himself as on his day off. Maybe he'd wanted to be a headwaiter at one time, but his father had died and left him the pawnshop. There's money in that, either way you played it, honest or under the table. Paul did a bit of both.

"Some soup, Jim?"

I shook my head. "With your money, you ought to be eating at the Midnight Sun."

"It's not the money," Paul said. "I like to dine alone."

I laughed with him and pulled back a chair and sat down at one corner of his desk. "I need two pieces, Paul."

"Could be." He turned off the burner and carried the pot to the desk. He placed the pot on the blotter and ate from it with a small spoon. "Do they have to be A-1 clean?"

"Nothing that can be traced."

When he nodded a dribble of soup ran down his chin. ".38's?"

"Short barrel. Belly guns."

"Wait here." He took another spoonful of soup to hold him and then he went out and closed the door behind him. I leaned across the desk and stared down at the soup. Chicken noodle, of course.

He returned a couple of minutes later. He carried a wadded up brown paper sack under one arm. He placed the bag in front of me and walked across the desk and began eating his soup again.

"Shells?" I said without looking into the bag.

He leaned over, almost out of sight behind the desk and brought up a box. He reached out and placed the shells next to the bag.

"How much?"

"Both are good as new and the price is up."

"How much?"

"Three hundred."

"Two fifty," I said.

"Two seventy-five."

I got out the wad of bills and counted it out on the desk top. He counted it with me and when I'd reach $275, he doubled them and shoved them in his pocket. "For this price, if they don't work, I'll come back and jam one up you."

"They work grade A. My word on that."

I stood up and dropped the shells into the bag with the guns.

"Pleasure doing business with you, Jim."

"Let's hope so," I said.

At a store on Whitehall, one that ripped off blacks, I bought each of us a package of T-shirts and shorts. I had a pretty good idea what Hump wore but I had to guess with Edward.

And then I went looking for a pay phone.

I kept it short and simple to Art. At the end I could almost see Art's doubting grin. "Where are you now, Jim?"

"I'd rather not say. But not at my house."

"I could send a cruiser to sweep your place."

"Wouldn't do much good. I'm going to be moving. Old man Templeton looks toward the end. He's living on balls alone. It can't be but a couple of days. Until then, I'm going to be everywhere but where we're expected to be."

"If I can help, call me."

"One thing you can do. After Edward and his sister, the next in line to inherit is a grandson who's now in Italy. I've been checking and the kid's father isn't where he's supposed to be and there's no way of finding out where he is. He's ticketed for Rome but he might be in this country. Any way to check that with Federal Immigration?"

"Give me his name."

I did and then I headed back out of town. On the way I stopped at an all-night joint and bought some sandwiches and a case of under-the-table beer.

Edward was asleep in one of the beds. Only the light in the bathroom was on. I put the case of beer on the floor next to Hump and went back and got the underwear, the sandwiches, and the bag with the two pieces in it. From across the way, in the motel office, I thought I saw a flash of light, as if a shade had been drawn back. The old broad was checking us out.

Hump popped the tabs on a couple of beers. I left the sandwiches with him and carried my beer and the bag with the iron in it into the bathroom. I sat on the john cover and took out the shells and then the first piece. It was wrapped in heavy plastic. I unwrapped it and found that it was a Charter Arms piece, the one they called the Undercover Model. It had a two-inch barrel and weighed about a pound. It was chambered for five rounds.

Whoever'd packed the piece had made sure there was plenty of oil on it. I took a wad of toilet paper and wiped it clean. It looked to be in good shape: no rust, a few scratches but no damage I could see. More than likely it had never been fired. Probably a gun somebody'd bought to keep at home. And when the house got ransacked, the gun went along with the color TV and anything else that wasn't bolted down and had some value. The gun went to the same fence that handled the TV set and the other junk and, through an underground chain, it ended up in Atlanta.

I loaded the cylinder and put it aside.

The other piece was an S. & W. Centennial, a .38 on a .32 frame, with a two-inch barrel, double action only, chambered for five rounds, and it weighed a few ounces more than the Undercover Model. With the oil wiped away, it showed a bit more use, a few specks of rust. I loaded it and carried both pieces into the bedroom. I held them out to Hump. "Your choice."

"What's the difference?"

I held out the Charter Arms Undercover Model. "This one you can fire single action or double."

"Huh?"

"Oh, hell." I put the Undercover model into my jacket pocket and passed him the S. & W. Centennial. "This one you just point and pull the trigger."

Hump put it on the table near his elbow.

"Your next choice. Sleep now for four hours or take the first watch?"

"First watch," Hump said, "while the beer is still cold."

When he woke me, I felt like I'd been in a sandstorm and caught most of it under my eyelids. I had him wait a few more minutes. I had a hot shower and then a cold shower and dressed in clean underwear. There wasn't much I could do about the whiskers. At home it wouldn't have bothered me. Here, without a razor, it became a part of the crappy feeling of roughing it.

I had a ham and cheese sandwich and a warm beer while I listened to Hump shifting around in the bed, trying to find the comfortable part of it. Within a few minutes his deep snore joined Edward's thinner, breathier one.

I had the long part of the watch. I let them sleep until I saw the first slice of sunrise.

I shook each of them by the shoulder. "Up. It's time to move on."

"We could have stayed another day," Hump said.

"Maybe."

"Why not?"

"I don't like the accommodations."

The impulse to move on had come on me during the long night watch. I'd started trying to think like them, trying to figure how I'd go about searching for some men who didn't want to leave town and couldn't stay at their homes. And I knew I'd start checking the motels, the ones that were out of the way, off the main track. And I'd been right. I couldn't tell him in front of Edward but when I'd gone to drop off the key the old blonde had said, "I wasn't supposed to tell you, but your brother called."

"Huh?"

"If you want to see your brother you ought to wait."

"How long ago did he call?"

"About half an hour."

"He say anything else?"

"He said your wife wasn't mad anymore and you could come home."

"Bugger her," I said.

So we were taking a box step now. South down 85 to Newman. Highway 16 through Raymond, Sharpsburg, Senoia, and Digby, now swinging east. At Griffin, I bought a bag of ham biscuits and coffee to go. A toilet stop in Conyers before we took the state road to Loganville. Next Snellville and onto the Stone Mountain Expressway. Scott Boulevard to Decatur. An hour's layover in Decatur for lunch in a cafeteria where it seemed only auto mechanics ate. And from Decatur back into Atlanta on Ponce de Leon.

It was early afternoon and it was time to find us a hole deep in Atlanta and pull the edges in over us.

I stopped at a pay phone and while Hump and Edward stretched their legs, I put in a call to Beth Fanzia.

"Is Edward all right? I want to see him."

"Actually, that's why I called," I said.

After we talked, I went back to the car. Hump drove now. He dropped us on a corner out on Whitehall. It was near a bar, one of the early ones that opened about seven in the morning, and we went in and sat at the bar and drank a couple of drafts. I watched the street. Twenty minutes later Hump was back. It had been a fairly easy drill: a couple of circuits of the block where his apartment was, and when he was sure it wasn't being watched, a one-for-one trade, my car for his. Mine was getting too well known.

"What now?" Hump asked as he pulled away from the curb.

"What time's dark?"

"Something after seven o'clock."

"We've got to get lost," I said.

"I know a place."

I'd have thought it was a service station that had gone out of business. It wasn't. In back there were a couple of large rooms, in each room a half-dozen tables with chairs. Against one wall was an old drink box that might have been in a service station before the coin machines came in, and next to that an old juke box that must have gone back to the early fifties.

The fat black man watched Hump park so that the car was hidden from the road. When we reached him, he pushed the door to one of the rooms open. "Hump, there's a tall six in the drink box."

"The food?"

"Buckets of chicken on the table."

Hand on the roll of bills in my pocket, I leaned in close to Hump. "How much?"

"Fifty."

I peeled it off and handed it to him. Hump passed it to the black. "You haven't seen us, Oakly."

"That goes with it."

"I mean it," Hump said.

The black had been moving away. Now he came back. "I won't cross you, Hump."

"Thanks."

"Slap the lock on your way out."

Hump found a light switch near the door. When he flipped that, the lights of the juke box went on too. Edward left us and sat down at the table with the two buckets of chicken. Hump lifted the lid of the drink box and got out three tall Buds.

I checked the room. The windows had been painted black. There wasn't a back door, just the one we'd entered through. I didn't like that. But there wasn't much I could do about it. I sat down at the table and dug a chicken breast out of the open bucket. "An after-hours place?"

"Private parties."

"Kids?"

Hump wiped chicken grease off the rim of his beer can. "Kids who can't drink in the bars and clubs. That's anybody under eighteen."

"Good business?"

"A hundred a night. That includes a free juke box. It's weekends mostly."

"You trust him?"

"Oakly? Not much, but I sandbagged him some."

Edward stood up. He carried his beer over to the juke box. He pressed a button. The first record that played was the Bette Midler version of "Boogie Woogie Bugle Boy." After about half of the song had played, he turned to me. "You remember this one?"

"Barely," I said.

"The Andrews Sisters did it."

"You in the service back then?"

"A bit," he said. He swung around and leaned into the juke box light. I waited for him to add something to that but he'd closed us out.

✤ ✤ ✤

Around seven, I went outside and looked around. There were no cars but ours in the lot, nobody hidden along the sides of the building. I whistled and Edward and Hump came out. Edward was withdrawn now. He'd been that way since I'd asked him the question about time in the service. I couldn't bitch with that. He didn't have to like us. All he had to do was stay alive.

When we reached the Melton Towers, I pulled into the driveway. As soon as I braked, Hump had the door open. He was out, an arm around Edward's shoulders, running him into the lobby. Beyond them, in the lobby, I could see the strained face of Beth Fanzia.

As soon as Edward was inside, Hump ran back out to the car. So far so good. Edward would be in the elevator, on his way up to the kind of security that only a few million dollars can buy.

I parked in a lot down the street. "You think we're clear?"

"So far."

"Odd." It was goose-pimple time. "This is one place I'd watch."

"Too many places," Hump said. "Plus all that chasing around on the back roads."

We left the parking lot and stopped at the curb, waiting for a couple of cars to pass so that we could cross. When the alley opened up, we trotted across the street, angling so that we approached the Towers. I was in the driveway when I turned and looked back. I'd intended to check the other side of the street. But a black Buick passed close to us, and the man in the passenger seat was illuminated for just a brief moment. I didn't get a good look but I got a flash of something white on his face, adhesive tape showing below a hat or a small bandage.

The knife man I'd hit with the ash tray? I couldn't be sure.

"Something wrong?"

I told him. "I think we've blown it."

The goose pimples didn't leave me for almost an hour.

# CHAPTER FIVE

ifteen minutes later, Hump and I were in the Elizabeth Barrett Browning living room. Beth entered from a bedroom beyond about the time we arrived. She was dressed in black now, and it might have been a harsh judgment on my part, but I had the feeling she was rehearsing for a funeral. The old man couldn't have much life left in him.

Even in black she looked good. All that prime, aged meat. It was getting to me even though I knew that young was better and that she probably hadn't noticed that I had a fly or a zipper.

She asked if I'd make the drinks and I did the best I could. Scotch on the rocks for Hump and me, and gin with a drop of vermouth and a lemon twist for her. I'd lost track of the time but I guessed that it must be the cocktail hour.

"Edward looks terrible," she said when I handed her the drink.

"He's alive. The hard fact is that he'd look a lot worse dead."

"You can be crude." It wasn't a knock the way she said it. It was more like a realization.

"Can't change my lifestyle now," I said.

Hump asked where Edward was now.

"He's in with Daddy."

I should have known that. A death scene out of some Russian novel, that was natural enough. I sipped the Glenlivet and looked around the room. There wasn't a phone in sight.

"I need to make a call."

"There's one in my bedroom." She tipped her head toward the doorway through which she'd entered.

"And I'll need to talk to the head of security here at the Towers. I want him to bring the personnel folders on all the men who will be working the shifts here for the next two or three days."

"Is that usual?"

"I don't know. He might not like it. Have Foster do it. He knows how to throw the power around."

"Yes, *Mr.* Hardman."

I winked at her and went into the bedroom. It was in blues, lights and darks played off against each other. And through a doorway beyond I could see a bathroom in black tile. I sat on the edge of the double bed and dialed the Department number and asked for Art.

"You?"

"It's me. You check out Count Fanzia for me?"

"Three days ago he landed at Kennedy. He was in New York for a day and a half and flew out late yesterday, back to Rome."

"He could have been talking killing with somebody up there."

"Maybe," Art said. "Here's something else for your scrapbook. How much do you know about Edward Templeton?"

"Not much."

"Then I'm one ahead of you. He's a deserter."

"A what?"

"Thirty years ago, 1943, he was an ensign in the navy. He was supposed to ship out from Treasure Island near San Francisco. He missed the ship."

"You sure of this?"

"I'm sure."

"Well, it doesn't have anything to do with what we're working on," I said.

"Statute of limitations would have run out anyway."

"It doesn't sound like something he'd do. Of course, I don't know him that well."

"Hard to say what somebody'd do." I heard a noise on the line like the flick of a lighter. "Where are you now?"

"Melton Towers."

"You going to hole up there?"

"As long as it's safe."

"You might have a day or so before they know you're there," Art said.

"Maybe not. We might have been seen going in."

"That's tough. The best security in the world can't protect him if somebody wants to run the money up."

That was true. It was the kind of truth I didn't want to think about.

We started dinner without Edward. Hump and Beth sat on one side of the table, facing Foster and me. A soup with the tang of lemon and slivers of chicken in it was followed by a grilled sole and then roast veal. Edward came in during the meat course and passed up everything else. He looked tired and red-eyed.

I couldn't look at him in quite the same way. The knowledge I had about the desertion thirty years before shaded the way I saw him. I suppose that was because World War II had been the last of the popular wars. It was easy to understand why some kid in the late 1960's didn't want to show up for the Nam one. But No. 2 had been a different matter. We'd been the good guys in that one. Staying out of it, deserting, was like putting yourself on the side of the gas ovens and the worldwide bloodbath.

I knew I'd have to deal with this feeling somehow. Protecting him would be hard enough. If I let myself start thinking he wasn't worth protecting, we could end up with a funeral or two.

After coffee and Benedictine, Hump and Foster and I left Edward and Beth still over their coffee and walked through the maze of hallways into the living room that opened out into the foyer where the elevators were. It was the one I thought didn't look lived in. A man in a dark suit waited there for us. He stood at a kind of relaxed attention, a lean man, tanned, with a brush cut to his sun-bleached hair and the pale shadow of a scar on the right side of his neck. Gun burn, I decided.

"Mr. Cleland," Foster said, introducing him.

His handshake had a few hours of repressed anger in it. Even after I wanted to pull my hand away, he held it, grinding the knuckles together. I didn't show that it hurt. Still, Hump noticed and when I introduced them, they held hands so long it looked like they might be falling in love. It was, from the way both acted as they stepped apart, at least a draw.

"Did you bring the personnel records?"

"I did," Cleland said to Foster. Turning, he lifted a thin stack of file folders from a chair seat behind him. He handed them to Foster and Foster passed them to me.

"Thank you," Foster said.

Cleland couldn't let it go. Since he was probably an honest man, with a good reputation in security, I could understand his position. "I'm afraid someone here owes me an explanation. I've been in charge of security here at Melton Towers since it opened about eight years ago. In that time there has been no incident that..."

"It's a special case," I said. "As far as I know there's been no doubt about the security here."

Foster said, "This time it's a matter of life or death. At least, Mr. Hardman has convinced me of that."

"I still want an explanation," Cleland said.

"And I'll be glad to give you one." I handed the file folders to Hump. "Put these in the bedroom. I'll look through these after I've had the tour with Mr. Cleland."

"You don't need me?"

"Stay close to Edward."

He nodded and Cleland and I left Foster and Hump in the living room and entered the foyer. A young guard sat at the desk there. There was a phone on one corner of the desk and a Thermos bottle on the floor near his feet.

Cleland started the tour. He stopped next to the desk. "Anyone coming up from the lobby has to be okayed from below." He leaned over the desk and withdrew a large ledger from the right-hand desk drawer. "Each day the ledger is filled in. Who is expected and when. Any visitors who try to get to this floor who aren't on the ledger would be referred to Mrs. Fanzia or to Mr. Foster, if he's here. Only after the visitor is cleared is he allowed into the elevator, accompanied by one of the main-door guards. That guard has a key that will open the elevator doors at this floor."

"A master key?"

He said yes.

"What's to keep someone from getting clearance to the eighth floor, and then, once they're on the elevator, drawing a gun and forcing the guard to go beyond that and open the doors to the twelfth?"

"Only the security procedures below."

"Single keys would be better, a key for each floor. The guard, when he brings a man up to the eighth floor, couldn't be forced to open some other door."

"Perhaps. On the other hand, that many keys would be confusing."

I let it go for the time. I could see that he was going to reject any suggestion I made. I nodded at the young guard at the desk. "What if he has to piss or something?"

"He calls downstairs and says he'll be off the desk for a minute or two. When he returns he calls back in."

"Is there a stairwell?"

"Over there." Cleland pointed toward a door to the right of the foyer. "It can be operated either by a buzzer here at the desk or a key the guard keeps on a ring."

"What's to keep someone from getting off on the floor above or below this one and reaching that stairwell door?"

"Nothing, but they wouldn't be able to get in."

"They might pick the lock."

Cleland grinned at me, a grin without warmth or amusement in it. "There's no lock to pick on that kind of door."

I followed him to the elevator. He inserted a key. While we waited for the elevator I asked, "Is that a master too?"

"Yes."

"So that means there are two masters."

"Three," he said. "One is locked in my safe, back at the office."

We rode the elevator down to the lobby. As soon as we stepped out, the two main door guards straightened up a red hair or two. Cleland nodded at them and unlocked a door just to the side of the main entrance. A uniformed guard looked up at us as we walked in. He was seated in front of a control board. In the panel in front of him there was a single TV monitor. We stood behind him and watched while he turned a selector knob. It was like changing channels on a home TV set. Only this time he was checking the entrance foyers of floors one through twenty. He hesitated a few seconds at each floor, just long enough to make a notation in the log. On the fourteenth floor the guard was smoking a cigarette. Cleland grunted and touched the guard on the shoulder before he turned the selector knob.

"Make a note for him."

"Elliot," the guard said.

"If I catch him smoking at the desk one more time, he's out."

"Yes, sir."

As we left the control room, the guard was making a note on a pad. Out in the lobby, Cleland said, "With any coordination at all, Elliot should be able to piss and smoke at the same time. Smoking on duty looks sloppy."

I nodded. He seemed to have it running like a military outfit. "Is there a back entrance?"

"What they call the trade entrance. It's open from nine to four. While it's open, there's a guard on duty and all deliveries are checked before they're received. No deliverymen are allowed beyond the checkpoint. Every hour deliveries are made to the floors by a guard using the trade elevator."

"No way they could get through that entrance now?"

"Any tampering with the trade door sets off a silent alarm in the control room. And even if they got past the rear door, they would not be able to use the trade elevator or enter the lobby." He raised an eyebrow. "Would you like to inspect that entrance?"

I shook my head. "It's like Fort Knox."

He led the way back to the elevator. Before he inserted the key, he put his back to the doors. "I think it's time you explained what this is all about."

"That's fair." I told him about the attempts on the life of Edward Templeton. He listened, without interrupting me, his eyes hard on me. At the end he grunted and said, "Mr. Templeton pays for and expects the best. The problem is that this security system wasn't designed to handle that kind of try."

"It looks pretty tight to me."

"It's designed to handle pests and to protect an old lady from being mugged in the elevator by someone who just walked in off the street. It's not geared to handle a professional try."

There was no use lying about it. He was right. "Two weaknesses I see. The master keys the guards use."

"I can't do anything about that now," Cleland said.

"The other one is the two guards at the main entrance. If someone has to be escorted to one of the floors that leaves only one man in the lobby."

"I can add another man within the hour. The expense, of course, will have to …"

"Bill Mr. Templeton for that."

Cleland inserted the key and the elevator doors opened. "A real hard try with automatic weapons might get past the lobby."

"Not if you tell the men what to expect."

"I don't like this at all."

I said I couldn't say that I was in love with it either.

He dropped me off at the twelfth floor and checked me past the guard in the foyer.

The room they'd furnished us was in the suite furnished to Edward. His room was next to ours. There were twin beds and Hump, fully clothed, was stretched out on one.

There was a table and I sat there for an hour and went through Cleland's files. You could say this for him. The background checks he did would have rated pretty well with the F.B.I. When I'd put the last file aside, I still hadn't found a flaw. I'd looked for any man who'd been hired recently, but that was a dead end. All the men on the job had been employed for six months or longer.

I tapped the files together until they were in a neat stack. "How's Edward?"

"Sleeping like a baby, the last time I looked."

"Keep an eye open. We'll set up watches later."

I carried the files through the halls and out to the foyer. I had the desk guard call down for Cleland and then I waited until he came up. I returned the files to him. He said he was leaving now that the extra guard was on duty down in the lobby.

I left him and went looking for a drink.

I found a bar in a small library near Beth Fanzia's living quarters. One thing you could say for the rich. They kept the liquor store cash registers ringing, especially the high dollar keys. I looked over the bar and passed up the Glenlivet this time in favor of the bourbon. Lord, it was good. Smoother than Jack Daniels Black and aged a few years longer than Wild Turkey. I couldn't tell from the decanter what it was, unless it was some kind of private stock. Sipping it straight, seated in a soft chair, I decided when the job was over, I'd try to find some way of making off with a bottle or two of it.

"Is this the way you protect Edward?"

Beth Fanzia was in the doorway. There was a book in one hand. The other hand held together the neck of a no-nonsense robe, a practical robe, no see-through, made out of a soft wool.

"He's protected right now." I held up the glass. "I'm protecting myself from the chill."

It hadn't been an accusation anyway, just her way of starting a conversation. Maybe the very rich have a hard time of just saying hello.

"I feel the chill myself." She passed me, holding the book out like she'd like to shelve it. She couldn't decide where it belonged, so she dropped it on a table. "What are you drinking?"

"The bourbon."

"Daddy's special reserve. I'll have some too."

I stood up. "Ice or water?"

"Are you drinking it straight?"

"Water's a sin in this," I said.

"Your way then," she said.

I brought over the decanter and a glass. She sat down in a chair across from mine. Now both of her hands were busy, one clutching the robe at the throat and the other holding the bottom edge closed across her knees. I grinned to myself and poured her a couple of knuckles of bourbon in the glass. I held the glass out to her. When she hesitated, not sure which part of the robe to let fall open, I laughed.

"Like they say at the Chicken Shack—breast or leg?"

That got her pride up. "Which do you prefer, Mr. Hardman?"

"Jim," I said. "Both or either or neither."

She released the top of the robe and I got my look at her breasts then, right down to the nipples. I was still having trouble putting it together, the guess I had of her age and the way she'd held the body together. It might be will but it was also a matter of a hell of a lot of exercise.

"See enough?" She took the drink.

"For now." I backed away and sat down.

"You're no gentleman." The first few sips of bourbon put a flush of color in her face.

"That's the second time I've heard that this week. The other time it was from your father."

"From him," she said, "that's a high compliment."

"And from you?"

"Half and half."

"You like sitting on fences?"

"Not as much as I like men," she said.

"How many have there been?"

"Husbands? Or do we count lovers as well?"

"We could start with husbands and go on from there."

"Three," she said.

"Run them down for me."

"My first was an All-America tackle from Tennessee. He made love like he played football, mean and hard." She smiled at the thought. "It was fine if you didn't mind the bruises the next day."

"A tackle is a fullback with his brains kicked out," I said.

"Does that mean anything?"

"No."

"My second was Count Fanzia. It seemed the thing to do at the time. He had a name and no money and I had money and not much left of a name."

"Too much high living?"

"You should have known me in London and Paris."

"And what happened with the Count?"

"He was a lot of man, but after Rudolph was born he lost interest in me. He had, situated all over Italy, a number of other interests."

"The continental view of life," I said. "So you got your feelings hurt and moved on to number three."

"A charming man. A man who could do everything well but make a living. Do you know he could order a whole meal in Chinese?"

"That must have been pretty impressive, at least once a month."

"He was, to be sure, a few years younger than I was."

"How few?"

"Eight, I think. The problem was that he seemed confused about our relationship at times. It was as if he thought I was his mother. Can you believe that?"

"He was a mixed-up boy," I said.

"Wasn't he, though?" She'd finished the couple of knuckles of bourbon. Either the bourbon or the talk about husbands had softened her. Something had happened. And I liked it enough not to question it.

I picked up the decanter from the rug at my feet and stood up. I leaned over her and poured a splash more into her glass. I put the decanter aside and waited. The temptation was in me. And while she drank, she watched me over the rim of the glass, a trace of a smile on her lips.

As soon as she lowered the glass, I took it out of her hand. She didn't protest. Either she'd read my mind or she'd played the same scene so many times she knew all the lines.

I put the glass next to the decanter and reached out and grabbed the top of the robe. She closed her eyes then and the eyelids flickered when I put out my hands and caught her breasts in my palms. Firm, good weight, with the nipples rubbing against my hands.

"You surprise me, Mr. Hardman." It was a soft, faraway voice.

"Jim," I said.

"Jim." Her hand fumbled at me. After it touched my belt it moved down and stroked the front of my fly. She didn't have any trouble finding me. I leaned closer and I was just kissing her when the light went out. I might not have noticed that. There wasn't any way to ignore the blast of a shotgun and the burb-burp-burp of an automatic weapon.

# CHAPTER SIX

I said, "Down on the floor, Beth." I took my hands away from her breasts and caught her by the shoulders. "Stay flat on the floor and don't move until I come back."

"Jim..."

I jerked her out of the chair and dumped her on the floor. So much for tenderness. I turned and ran for the door, where I thought the door was. I hit the frame with a shoulder and kept going. It staggered me some but I got the .38 out and put the hammer back on cock. I was moving as fast as I could, with one hand sliding down the hallway wall, feeling for a doorway. I found the doorway and turned left. I was trying to run a film through the back of my mind, trying to see the halls and the rooms as I ran. In the film the hall was longer than it really was. I hit a closed and locked door before I realized it was there. I hit it hard enough to bounce back. It was luck for me that I did.

A round slammed into the door, off to the side. It was a pistol shot, not the shotgun or the automatic weapon.

"Goddamit, Hump..."

"Jim?"

"Shit, yes."

I heard movement and the lock sliding open.

"Jim, look, I'm sorry..."

I pushed past him. "Where's Edward?"

The raspy voice answered me. "Over here."

"Good." I reached out and caught Hump by the arm. "You know how to load the piece?"

"Sure."

I dug into my jacket pocket and brought out a few shells. "Here. Replace the round you just fired." I dumped the shells into his hand.

"Where you going?"

"I've got to see what's going on. It sounds like a shotgun and a grease gun."

"Watch yourself."

"You and Edward stay on the floor. Heads down."

I backed out of the door. Hump followed me that far. Before he closed the door between us, I said, "Don't open the door for anybody but me."

"Luck."

Then the lock slid into place and off in the distance I heard the next burst of gunfire. This time it was a shotgun, three bursts so fast the echoes overlapped. I stopped in the hall, listening. No more gunfire. I waited until I was fairly certain that I had the layout clear in my mind. I'd just left Beth's suite and nobody'd reached Edward's yet. That left the old man's living quarters and the living room and the foyer where the desk guard was.

I took it slow. I didn't want to blunder into a shotgun or a Sten gun. And if those shotgun blasts or the burp blasts had hit anyone, they weren't going to be any deader if I got there a few minutes later.

When I reached the end of the hall that led to the old man's suite, I stopped long enough to untie my shoes and step out of them. I carried them with me. It was quieter going but the floor had been waxed and buffed recently and I knew I was going to have tired arches from trying to grip the slippery surface.

I was a few feet from the outer living room door of the old man's suite when it was briefly outlined by a flash of light. The light also revealed a white figure sprawled in the hall just ahead of me. Then the light was gone. I moved forward, ticking off the distance in my mind. I reached the figure and bent over it. One touch and I knew that it was the huge nurse I'd seen on my first visit to the old man's hospital-like room. I could tell that from the starchy feel of the cloth. I found her head and moved my hand down to her neck. No pulse. She was dead. I stepped over her and felt my right sock get wet. I'd stepped into her blood.

I flattened myself against the wall and waited. I could hear voices.

"Shit, Ernie, we got the wrong man. This is some old fucker."

"No, shit, no, this was the right room."

"Look, you dumb-ass..."

I grabbed the molding on the door frame, ducked low and swung myself into the living room. I could see the hospital bedroom straight ahead, illuminated by the strong beam of a flashlight.

"If this is the wrong guy, then where the fuck is...?"

I moved to the left, clearing the doorway. I couldn't see where I was going. I put out a hand and touched something. It moved away from me. I grabbed for it but it rolled out of my reach. And then I realized I'd set a wheelchair in motion. It was rolling toward the bedroom. I got on my knees and crawled. I wanted to get out of the line of fire if the two men were jumpy. I got a few feet away from the doorway before the wheelchair struck a table. A lamp fell and shattered. I flattened out and dug my toes into the rug.

The flashlight swept across the living room and the grease gun stitched its way across the wall above me, showering me with plaster and wood debris.

"Jumpy, Ernie?"

"Up you."

The light reflected off the wall enough for me to see that I'd positioned myself behind a brocaded sofa. I took my breaths in small bites of air, nothing they could hear.

"Where's Walk? He's supposed to be here."

"It's gone bad," the other one said.

The two men moved toward the doorway that led to the hall. I still couldn't see them. The light was pointed down now, wagging its way across the carpet. I could have fired and I might have got one or both of them. I let them go. A pistol wasn't much against a pump shotgun and a grease gun. The odds weren't right. As they neared the doorway, the light cut toward the right and they moved off in that direction. I didn't like it. That meant they were going toward the suite where Hump and Edward Templeton were. The only thing Hump and Edward had going for them that I didn't was that they were behind a thick door and they'd been warned to stay low on the floor. They might weather it.

I got to my knees. I reached for the curled armrest at the end of the sofa and I was pulling myself up when another light cut through the darkness. The beam was directed toward the bedroom. "Ernie? You in here?" A man followed the light into the living room. The light was steady on the mess in the bedroom for a long count and then the hand shifted and the light began a slow sweep of the room.

Just enough time. I took the careful stance, with my left hand locked over my right wrist to steady it. I still couldn't see him. I had to guess. I sucked in a slow breath and shot him three times as fast as I could drag the trigger.

He yelled when the first one hit him. And at least one of the other two hit him about heart high. The flashlight jerked out of his hand, hit the carpet, and bounced and rolled. Something else, something heavier, dropped out of his other hand and struck the floor about the time his body did.

I scooped up the flashlight and turned it on him. He was dead and for a moment I thought it had gone wrong. The man with the hole torn in his chest was wearing a policeman's uniform. But the panic passed. I remembered that he'd called for Ernie. That meant he wasn't a cop. I could breathe again then.

I switched off the light and grabbed him by one leg and tumbled him out of the doorway. When he was off to one side I felt around the carpet until I found the weapon he'd been carrying, a wicked-looking double-barreled shotgun with the barrels cut down. I had to use the light again. I pointed it away from the door and held the shotgun in the beam. I broke the shotgun and checked the shells. Both unfired. I replaced the shells and put the shotgun on the floor at my feet. While I waited, I replaced the three rounds I'd fired from the .38. I switched off the flashlight. I was ready.

I put it together this way: the one I'd shot was probably the guy, Walk, the other two had mentioned. He'd been stationed out in the foyer. By the timetable he'd been scheduled to join them and hadn't. And when he'd arrived, the other two had already left to try to do the real job the contract called for. They were pros. Anyone else would have seen that the job had gone rank and would have pulled out. Not these. They were trying to salvage it.

They must be nervous now, with second thoughts. They'd heard the three rounds I'd fired. It meant somebody was behind them, between them and the way out. If they didn't like it, neither did I. What had given me the edge on Walk had been surprise. That wasn't with me anymore. When they came back down that hallway they'd be wary. Watchful.

So I waited. I didn't like the smells, what death really smelled like. Blood and crap and piss.

Off in the distance the pump gun bit first, three or four rounds as fast as he could pump it. And it was joined and over-lapped by the *rupt, rupt, rupt* of the grease gun. I held my breath. I didn't have to hold it back long. As the echoes died down, I heard the lower bite of Hump's .38. The pump gun answered Hump and the grease gun added in a fifteen- or twenty-round burst. Silence. I counted. I reached twenty-five before I heard them running. The footfall getting louder as they came toward me. One of them was gagging for breath. The beam of their light wagging from wall to wall.

I placed the flashlight on the floor, angling it so that it would point down the hall that led to the living room behind the foyer.

I'd be leading them with the light. The timing had to be perfect. There was only about twenty-five feet of hallway left after they passed the doorway where I'd be. After that there was an elbow breaking to the right.

As they passed the doorway I reached down and found the button on the flashlight. When I switched it on, it froze them.

"Walk…" one began.

They were shoulder to shoulder, turning, facing into the strong light. "That you, Walk?"

"Yeah," I grunted.

The light one of them held angled toward the doorway. It was getting close when I placed the sawed-off shotgun against my shoulder and pulled trigger for both barrels.

It was a pig-killing, a slaughterhouse.

Within a few minutes Art and a squad arrived from the Department. I laid it out for him. He made notes while I walked through it with him. We were in the living room, where I'd killed the first man, when Cleland came steaming down the hall. He was being hassled all the way by a uniformed cop whom Art had left in the foyer.

Cleland saw me and said, "I am not going to take the responsibility for this … this."

"You talk to your men?"

After I'd got over the last two killings, I'd gone out into the foyer and found the desk guard knocked out and taped up. The single guard who'd come up with them in the elevator was sprawled next to the open elevator doors. He'd been badly beaten and a lump on the back of his head was still bleeding.

That was as far as I went until Art called from below. By that time the desk guard was all right and I sent him down with the elevator to bring Art up. Art told me what he'd found downstairs.

They'd found the two guards who'd been left at the main door to the lobby in the electronic control room. Those two, as well as the one operating the television board, had been taken like innocent children.

Cleland nodded. He had talked to his men.

"You hire them for their stupidity?"

"They were wearing police uniforms."

"Sure they were," I said.

"They said there'd been a report of a robbery on the ninth floor." Cleland swallowed. "They seemed to be ..."

"Of course they seemed. That's what the whole operation was based on."

"You police?" Cleland asked Art. I guess he'd had enough of me.

"Yeah," Art said.

"Where'd they get those uniforms?"

Art shrugged. "We're going to find that two or three cleaners got hit early this evening, ones that handle a lot of police uniforms. We'll know which ones in a day or two, when the policemen go by to pick up their uniforms and the cleaners can't find them."

"I need to talk to someone in authority," Cleland said.

"Foster's back with Mrs. Fanzia," I said.

Art watched him stalk away. "You know how to hurt a guy, don't you?"

"That stupid shit. I told him there might be a try. The least he could have done was leave orders for them to call up here as soon as anything out of the ordinary happened."

"If they had time. I don't think they did." Art looked at the peppered and blasted walls in the old man's room. "You've got to admit it looked good."

"Sure," I said, "and all cops carry grease guns as standard issue."

"They didn't see a grease gun," Art said.

I nodded toward the sawed-off shotgun on the floor where I'd left it. "That looks like a riot gun too, doesn't it?"

The markings were chalked on the floor. The outlines of the body, and out in the hallway other markings. But the bodies were gone. It helped some, but I still wasn't sure I was past losing my dinner. The charges of Double-O buck in the narrow hall, from a distance of only a few feet, had splattered them all over the walls. The splatterings were still there, looking like some child had thrown his spaghetti dinner against the white plaster.

A plainclothes cop I didn't know called Art from the hallway. When Art came back, he held out a sheet of paper. "This was found on the body of the one you got first."

It didn't take long to figure it out. The page was divided into two parts. The bottom half was a scale drawing of the downstairs lobby, the main door, the control room, and the elevator. The top half of the page covered the floor we were on: the elevator, the foyer, the unused living rooms, and the hallway that led to the old man's suite of rooms. There was a big X marked where the hospital-like room was.

"Somebody screwed it up," Art said.

"It looks that way." I handed the paper back to him.

"It won't make the old man feel any better, but you'd better be glad they fucked up. Otherwise you and Hump and the Templeton guy might be dogmeat now."

I didn't tell him that I wouldn't have been with Hump and Edward. That I'd had my hands full of titty and a hard-on when the shooting started.

Maybe Art could guess I was holding back something. He flipped back to the first page of his notes. "You didn't say exactly where you were when the war kicked off."

"Down the hall."

"With Hump?"

"Not that hall," I said.

"Off duty?"

"Having a drink with a lady."

Art laughed. If he'd known the rest of it, he'd have laughed even harder.

After Art left, I worked my way through the rooms and the halls until I found Hump and Edward. On the way I stopped off for another look at the bedroom where Hump and Edward had been. The door had been blown almost off its hinges.

Hump and Edward were in the small library where I'd left Beth. Foster was there also. Beth came in about the time I did. I could see the red eyes and the puffiness. Even though she'd been expecting the death of her father, she'd been unprepared for the sudden way it had happened.

I nodded at Foster and Edward and sat down next to Hump. There was a bandage on the back of his right hand. "Trouble?"

"A splinter from the door," he said. "I kept my head down but my hand was up."

Foster cleared his throat. He'd been waiting for me, I guess, and now he wanted me to end my conversation with Hump. I looked over at him.

"Mr. Hardman, I think we all know that you've done an excellent job."

I stood up and headed for the bar. "I'm not so sure about that." I found the bourbon decanter and poured myself about a fist of it. "If I'd done a good job Mr. Templeton wouldn't be dead."

"It could have been a lot worse." He indicated Edward and Beth.

"I don't think Cleland would agree with you."

"I've talked with him. He's angry, to say the least. He believes that by bringing Edward here you've made his air-tight security plan for the building look bad. You've hurt his reputation."

"Cleland depends too much on television," I said.

"I agree," Foster said. "And as soon as his contract expires in the next couple of months, I will have something to say about the security arrangements."

Too bad. But Cleland didn't seem to be flexible enough for the business. Screw him.

"And as I was saying just before you entered, I feel that the death of Mr. Rufus Templeton has changed our aspect somewhat. There is no reason to continue this guard for Edward. The inheritance has passed on to Edward. There is now no reason for anyone to harm him."

"That's shortsighted," I said.

"What?"

"We still don't know that someone was trying to kill Edward to keep him from inheriting. It could be something else. Anything else."

"Do you have any ideas?"

I didn't. I shook my head. It wasn't worth arguing. "Which means we're out of work."

Foster nodded. "If you'll list your expenses and bring them by my office…"

"Monday," I said. I stood up and nodded at Hump. "Ready?" I tossed back about two ounces of the bourbon and put the glass on the sideboard.

Beth came over to me. Since I'd left her, she'd put on a black dress and there was no memory on her face of what had almost happened. She took my hand. "We do appreciate what you've done for us."

Killed three men.

"I tried," I said, "and I'm sorry about your father."

I let her hand go and Hump and I nodded at the others in the room. We went down the hall to the blasted-up bedroom. We hadn't brought much with us and there wasn't much to take away. I'd worn a light topcoat and the last time I'd seen it, it had been over the back of a chair. Now the chair was on the floor and the topcoat, when I lifted it, had a couple of bullet holes in the back. So much for what I'd brought with me. I'd add the coat to the expense list if I could remember what I'd paid for it about two years before at Davison's.

Edward was waiting for us out in the hallway. "I didn't want to talk in front of them."

I could understand that. I didn't much like talking in front of Foster, either.

"I think I owe both of you a lot."

"A day's work," I said.

"I don't believe that," Edward said.

"I guess I'm down," I said. I was. I was turning it back against myself, the cutting edge.

"The killings?"

I nodded.

"I'm sorry about those too," Edward said. "No matter what kind of men they were, I don't think my life is worth three of theirs."

"Well, it's done."

Edward walked out to the foyer with us. A different security man called up the elevator for us. Just before we stepped into it, we shook hands, Hump and Edward and then Edward and me. Edward said for us to come and visit him, but I think all three of us knew that we wouldn't. Edward had come into big money. He might not think it made any difference but it would. Money would close the doors around him. It always would.

We had a couple of hours in the bars before they closed at 3 a.m. Then we stopped at my place and drank some more. And we were still at it when the sun came up.

It was Saturday morning and I felt dead inside.

# CHAPTER SEVEN

My girl, Marcy, got back from San Francisco late Sunday afternoon. I think, during the morning, I remembered that I was supposed to meet her flight. By the afternoon I didn't remember much of anything except once when I tripped over a beer can and almost broke a leg. Or was it my hip?

She waited at Hartsfield for half an hour and then she called. She said later the phone was busy. I knew better. The phone had been off the hook for about a day. When she couldn't reach me, she took a cab from the airport straight to my house. It must have cost a fortune. She'd never tell me how much. That was the anger that burned right through my offer to pay her back the cab fare.

I guess I got off easy after all. She gave me hell for about ten minutes and then she made me some coffee and spent an hour cleaning up the top layer of the mess I'd made since the Templeton job had cranked down late Friday night.

Deserving it, I took it and didn't argue back. It was a good thing Hump wasn't around to get his share of it. He'd been on the toot with me. Or maybe, since I knew him well, he'd gone along with me to keep me out of trouble and out of the slammer. It wasn't what I set out to do, but I guess it was my way of salting down the ghosts of the three men I'd killed. If I ground myself down into fine enough powder, the three men didn't matter. At least it seemed to work that way.

Around seven o'clock, when I passed through the bedroom on the way to the john, Marcy was on the phone. I didn't know at the time, but she had called Hump and he'd told her about my two or three days of work. When I came out a couple of minutes later she was off the phone. She was standing at the foot of the bed, already undressed down to her half slip and bra.

I let her take me to bed, just holding me at first. And when the warmth rolled over me like hot oil, a violent, harsh love-making that didn't last long. A brief fire that burned each of us and then the quiet afterwards. And still a little drunk, at some level near the feverish nightmare, I felt the dead things in me gush out, as if my pores had opened to let them out. Washed out, clean. And then we slept for a couple of hours.

By eleven we were up and in the kitchen. Marcy was fixing us omelets with mushrooms and a side dish of asparagus. I sat and watched her and worked at the expense sheet I'd have to turn in to Foster the next day. There were some problems. The going rate for killing a man or three men? The cost of the shells? Depreciation of my mental health?

In the end I threw all that out and did it straight.

| | |
|---|---|
| GAS (ESTIMATED) | $ 30.00 |
| TOPCOAT (DAMAGED BY GUNFIRE) | 90.00 |
| TWO PISTOLS (CONFISCATED BY POLICE) | 275.00 |
| MOTEL (ONE NIGHT) | 17.50 |
| HIDE-OUT RENT (PARTY ROOM) | 50.00 |
| FOOD (ESTIMATED) | $40.00 |
| MISCELLANEOUS | 00 00 |
| TOTAL | $502.50 |
| ADVANCE | $1000.00 |
| EXPENSES | 502.50 |
| BALANCE ON HAND | $ 497.50 |

While we ate the omelets and the asparagus and drank white wine, Marcy turned the expense sheet and read it slowly. Once or twice she smiled. Then she looked across the table at me. "I think miscellaneous is cute."

"I like it myself. I'm going to put it on all my expense sheets from now on."

She touched the sheet with her head. "Do you have vouchers for all of this?"

"Are you kidding? I have an honest face."

"Ha!"

I threw the stalky end of a piece of asparagus at her. And missed.

"Tell me about the men in Frisco."

"What men?"

Early fall wind in the oak outside my window. If the tree hadn't been there when I bought the house, I'd have had to plant it myself.

"All those stud social workers."

Hand on her stomach, I could feel the laugh building, a quiver at first and then the hard explosion.

"Oh, those!"

"I thought so. Tell me about them."

"All hung like mice," she said. "Little white mice with pink eyes."

"I thought you wouldn't tell me."

"White mice," she said.

And then we slept.

Monday was a working day. I dropped her early at her apartment and then I drove downtown and loafed around for a time. I had breakfast and several cups of coffee. The main branch of the library opened at nine and I went in and looked at some librarian rear ends and read a few pages of a book on World War II airplanes.

At ten I drove straight down Peachtree to Colony Square. I didn't want to bother with the underground parking so I drove on past and left my car on 15th near the High Museum and walked back.

In the lobby of the office building I ran into Roger, Foster's black chauffeur. I shook his hand and started past him. He followed me to the elevator and said, "I've got to see you for a minute."

"Right now?"

"No, after you see Foster."

"The coffee shop downstairs?"

"There's a sandwich shop across the street."

I said I'd meet him there.

Foster's office was about as big as a tennis court. Or maybe two courts. Deep carpets. A desk, free form, shaped like an egg that had broken and run in a couple of directions. Racks of law books around the walls, but I was sure Foster never used them. Not with all those law clerks the firm had to do their scut work.

"Good to see you, Mr. Hardman," Foster said.

He leaned across the narrow part of the desk and gave me a limp handshake.

"It's Monday," I said.

"Yes, it is." He sat down and motioned me to a chair.

I passed him my neatly printed expense sheet. He ran a finger down the column without a pause. If he noticed my game with miscellaneous, he didn't show it. When he finished with the expense sheet, he drew a large circle around BALANCE ON HAND and put the sheet aside. "You have a balance of four hundred and ninety-seven dollars and some cents?"

I nodded. To be exact, that wasn't true. Hump and I had spent a bit over a hundred dollars of it partying.

"You were employed roughly for two days?"

It was a statement, not a question. I nodded.

Foster reached across the desk and pressed down the intercom button. "Miss Willis, bring in the Templeton estate checkbook." Leaning away, he said, "When we hired you, I'm not sure we were very exact on the subject of payment."

"I'm reasonable," I said.

"Of course, in the service there is what is called hazardous duty."

"I'm not sure that applies."

"I think it does."

Miss Willis brought in a large check register and placed it, open, in front of him. Before he wrote the check, he did some figuring on a scratch pad. Then he wrote the check. Passing it to me, he said, "You have a balance on hand of almost five hundred dollars. My check is for one thousand five hundred and two dollars and fifty cents. That will give you a total of two thousand dollars. Is that satisfactory?"

I said it was. And that it was generous as well.

He saw me out the door and I got the hell out of there before he changed his mind.

At Stan's Sandwich Shop across the street I got a cup of coffee and found Roger in the side room. He'd finished his coffee and now he was looking out at the street. I sat down across from him.

"You see Mr. Foster?"

"I saw him."

"He hire you again?"

I added some sugar to my coffee and just looked at him. "Run that by me again, Roger."

"He didn't hire you again?"

"He paid me off."

"The son of a bitch," Roger said.

I sipped my coffee. "Tell me about it."

"They buried Mr. Rufus Templeton yesterday. Somebody made another try at Edward after the funeral."

"How?" I lit a smoke.

"Outside the Towers as he was getting out of a car. A shot from a passing car. Used a silencer, I guess."

"Hit him at all?"

Roger shook his head. "Two shots, I think. One burned him on the arm. The other broke a glass in the car."

"You there, Roger?"

"No. I heard about it from the driver. He's a friend."

I leaned back and blew smoke at the ceiling. "Maybe Foster doesn't know. You sure he knows?"

"Not for sure. But it would be the first time he didn't know about something going on at the Templetons'. He keeps it under his thumb."

"Besides the money, what's his interest?"

"Mr. Foster got divorced about six months ago," Roger said.

"What does that mean?"

"I've got a feeling he wants to be Mrs. Fanzia's next husband."

"That wouldn't be hard work."

He grinned. "You too?"

"Just a passing interest," I said. "I don't want to buy the whole horse."

"The job's not done yet."

"What do you think I ought to do? I've been paid off and thanked and shown the door."

"There's Mrs. Fanzia."

"You think I ought to talk to her?"

He nodded. "That's what I'm thinking."

"She might not want to talk to me."

He said, "I know where she's going to be this afternoon."

"Where?"

"Lunch at that French restaurant on Luckie Street."

"Augustine's?"

"That's the place. She's going there at one o'clock."

"How long a lunch?"

"Usually an hour and a half."

I poured back the rest of my coffee and stood. "It's worth a try."

At the corner of 14th Street he crossed to Colony Square, heading for the underground parking. I waved at him and headed for 15th, where I'd left my car.

By two, I'd done a number of errands. I deposited the check and I went by Hump's and laid a couple of hundred on him, with the promise of more to come after the check cleared. And I'd stopped by Davison's and bought a replacement for the light topcoat that was in the trash now.

At two, I took up a position down the street from Augustine's. It was forty minutes later by my watch when the black Caddy turned off Forsyth and pulled to the curb in front of the restaurant. The driver, white, wearing the uniform and the cap, got out and walked around and stood with his hand on the passenger door handle. About five minutes later the door to Augustine's opened and three women came out. One of them was Beth Fanzia. The chauffeur removed his cap and swung the door open and I said, "Oh, shit," and started toward them at a fast walk. Only two of the women got into the Caddy and the one left on the walk was Beth. I slowed then and waited until the Caddy moved away from the curb.

She was dressed all in black, the mourning colors for her father. When I reached her, she was looking in the other direction, away from me. I said, "Beth."

I startled her. For an instant I thought she might faint.

"Jim."

When she turned to face me, I took her arm. "You have time for another drink?"

"Have you been following me?"

"Of course not," I said.

The bar had hardly opened. There were a couple of businessmen drinking their lunch and a tired hooker looking them over and trying to decide if they might be up for an afternoon roll. I got us J&B on the rocks at the bar and carried it over to the booth Beth had picked out.

She sipped hers and said, "How have you been, Jim?"

I shrugged. "I don't think we need to do any small talk."

"What's wrong?"

"I heard about the try on Edward yesterday."

"How did...?"

"It doesn't matter."

"I must be a vain old woman. I thought you'd gone out of your way to find me, just to find me."

It was an act. I was fairly certain of that. Maybe she'd been bothered by the interruption that night in the library the same way I had. But she didn't care a bit for me. It was a once-in-a-lifetime kind of magic and there wasn't any way to bring it back.

"That's a lot of crap, Beth, and you know it."

"As my father said and I said..."

"Why didn't you call me?"

"I didn't want to."

"Do better than that," I said. I reached across the table and caught her wrist. "Why?"

"I'm not supposed to tell you. He made me promise."

"Foster?"

"No, you fool, not Foster."

"Edward then?"

She nodded. She pulled her wrist away from me. "Yesterday, after it happened, I told him to call you. He said he wouldn't. I kept at him until he told me why. He said he wouldn't call you because he remembered your face, the way it was that night."

"When?"

"After you killed those three men."

"How did he say it was?"

"Empty, sick, bled down to the bone."

"Edward said that?"

"Exactly," she said.

"I'd have felt worse if he'd been killed."

"Edward's strange. I don't really understand him anymore. He doesn't think his life is worth all this death."

I said, "He didn't start this."

"That doesn't matter to him."

I finished my Scotch and swirled the ice around in the glass. "He up in the Tower?"

"Yes."

"You still have some of that good Glenlivet up there?"

"Yes."

"Invite me for a drink."

"Now?"

"Now," I said.

Having money hadn't changed him much. He wore the same kind of clothing except that he'd discarded his heavy work shoes for a pair of desert boots. They were still clean and new and he kept looking down at them as if he hoped they'd get dirty soon.

"I don't want this, Jim."

"I'd like for it to be over, too." I really didn't need the drink but I'd fixed Beth and me Glenlivets over ice. "So I want to make you a proposition, if you'll hear me out."

"I'll listen but I won't promise anything."

"Who's doing security for you now?"

"Cleland," he said.

"You satisfied?"

"I guess so."

"Then we'll leave it that way for the time." I poured a trickle of the Scotch onto my tongue and left it there. "And I want you to hire Hump and me. It might take a few days. It might take more than a week."

"Hire you to do what?"

"To go at it from the other end. Not to protect you. Better than that. To find out what this is all about. Who wants you dead and why."

He stared past me at Beth. I turned and saw the last part of a nod from her.

"And when you know?"

"I find a way to put a stop to it."

"No killing," Edward said.

"Without killing, if I can."

Beth walked past me, for a moment between us, and I think she must have nodded to Edward again. "I think you ought to do it," she said.

"All right, Jim, you're hired."

"But it's between us. You, Beth, Hump and me. Nobody else."

"Is that necessary?"

"I don't know. I'd like to think it isn't. It might be and I don't want anybody a step ahead of me all the way."

After we finished our drinks, Beth walked back to the foyer with me. At the elevator she asked, "Can you tell me where you'll start?"

"With your ex-husband."

She laughed. "Which one?"

"The Count. He has a motive and he was in New York for a bit over a day last week when he was supposed to be in Rome."

"I don't think he's capable of hiring a murder."

"There's one way to go about this: my way. I'm going to cull everybody I can. I'm going to narrow it down."

"I see."

"I might even check you out," I said.

"Damn you, Jim."

"Of course."

That night Hump and I took an Eastern flight to New York.

# CHAPTER EIGHT

After a night's sleep, I was out on the street early. The man I wanted to see wasn't in the phone book and I didn't know where he was living or what he was doing for money now. Still, I thought his schedule might be about the same. So I left messages for him. At a newsstand on Sixth Avenue, at an oyster and clam bar near Eighth Street and at a couple of sandwich shops.

The messages said I'd be in Herdt's Bar, the one behind the United Cigar Stand, just off Sheridan Square, from noon on.

From noon on, from the time Hump met me, we sat in the small bar and drank the Utica porter on tap. For lunch, Hump crossed the street to the deli and brought back huge sandwiches, thick with bloody roast beef.

It was a bit after two before Frankie showed up. By then we'd drunk so much of the porter that the bartender had just popped for one on the house. I didn't know him at first. He stood just inside the door, blinking and looking around. I recognized him when he grinned and came over to the booth.

He'd changed in the years since I'd seen him last. That had been some years before. He'd been a detective second grade then, a sharp dresser, a cop living above his income, liking the girls and good food and gobbling up a lot of both every year.

After the Knapp Commission, he was off the force and out on the street. As far as I know he hadn't done any slam time. Whatever had happened to him, a lot had gone down the time drain. He'd grown a beard, full but trimmed, and he'd given up suits for tight-fitting jeans and a faded denim jacket.

"Frankie." I pushed out of the booth and met him in the aisle and shook hands. Over my shoulder I nodded at Hump and introduced them. "You drinking?"

"I'll have what you are, if it's draft."

I nodded and went to the bar and got him a mug of porter.

He sat down next to Hump, across from me. "Draft's not bad for you. It's that pasteurized crap that hurts your system."

"You on nuts and berries now?"

"I'm giving it a try. You know, I haven't touched meat in over a year."

"It working?"

"It flushed my system out."

"How's Ellen?" The last time I'd seen Frankie he was into lifting weights. He'd even talked his wife Ellen into it. He was working out three days a week by himself and two days a week with her. I'd been surprised by what it had done to Ellen. I'd seen her in a low-cut blouse. She'd developed hard cords of muscle across her shoulders.

"Split last year."

"For good?"

"Probably. I don't even know where she is any more."

"What you doing for a living these days, Frankie?"

"Whatever comes along."

"I might have something for you."

He put his elbows on the table and leaned forward. "Tell me about it."

Hump excused himself and got out of the booth. He played about a dollar in the juke box. It was the old music, not that hard rock crap. I moved under the cover of the music and laid it out for him. When I finished and leaned away, he thought about it for a minute or two.

"Money in this?"

"Whatever it takes."

"I might have to use informers and that takes cash."

I nodded.

"Let me get this straight. You want to know if this Italian dude took out a contract on some guy down in Atlanta?"

"That's part of it. If he didn't, then who did?"

"You don't want much, do you?"

"Can do?"

"I can try." He held out a palm to me and I counted three hundred into it.

"If it takes more than this, use it and I'll make it good."

"Where can I reach you?" He tossed back the last of his porter.

"Here," I said. "Same time."

"Here?" He looked around. "You sleep here too?"

I shrugged. "I'm staying out of the cold wind."

"Even to me?"

I didn't say anything. Finally he nodded and said, "Better to be careful."

He waved at me and at Hump and left. We gave him ten minutes and then set out to see some of the town. Hump knew a girl and we took her along. I got drunk out and we didn't get to bed until after three in the morning. Rather, I got to bed at three. Hump left with the girl and didn't return until late breakfast time.

Waiting at the bar this time, I slowly sipped the first mug of porter and hoped the hangover would go away. Hump was in worse shape than me because of all that bareback riding.

The call came in at about 12:30 by the bar clock. I told the bartender yes, I was Jim Hardman and took the call in the pay booth.

"Jim, Frankie here. I might have something for you. It could cost you a couple of hundred."

"I've got the cash. Come on over."

"I can't right now," he said.

"When?" I looked over my shoulder. Hump was in the booth doorway, blocking it. I leaned toward him and let him put his ear close to the receiver.

"Tonight at ten."

"Where?"

"My place. You see, I don't think I ought to be seen with you. I've been asking questions and somebody might tag us together."

"Ten at your place? What's the address?"

He gave me a number on Eighth Avenue. "Ring the bell for apartment 8. The name's R. N. Snider. It's on the second floor. Got that?"

"I've got it."

"And come alone, Jim."

"Why's that?"

"You might look like fifty other people in town. But there just aren't that many nine-foot spades."

"Hump needs a night on the town anyway."

"Ten then," he said, "and bring the cash."

"Sure."

I hung up and we went back to our seats at the bar. I waved at the bartender and he brought over fresh mugs. After I'd paid him and he had moved back down the bar, Hump said, "How well do you know this Frankie dude?"

"I'm beginning to wonder."

"He might be trying to job you."

I grinned at him. "You don't want another night on the town?"

"Ten's not late. We finish our business by ten-thirty and we've got plenty of the night left."

"We could pass up the meet and make him come back to us."

"And always wonder about him?" Hump tipped back his head and poured down the whole mug of porter. And shuddered.

At ten of ten, a light cold rain was falling. It was like an Atlanta drizzle but with a sting to it. I was half a block down the street, in a doorway. We'd tagged the building earlier in the day in a slow-moving cab. It was a narrow shotgun building with a kind of gray shingle front. About fifteen minutes before, Hump had left me to work his way around the block and come in from the other direction. The way I figured it, if we'd been set up, they'd be watching me from a window above the street. If they saw me alone, they'd watch the street behind me to see if I was being followed. When they didn't see Hump, they'd decide that I'd bought the setup. After I entered Hump, would follow me in.

At five minutes to ten, I left the doorway and headed for the apartment building. I stayed near the curb, out in the wet splash of light. I acted some, hesitating now and then to read a house number, until I reached the shotgun building and read the number in the half moon of glass above the entranceway. There was a dim light in the small hall and a couple of rows of mailboxes and buzzers to the left. It was just enough light to read the names on the mailboxes. The name on Number 8 was, as Frankie had said it would be, R. N. Snider. I gave the buzzer a long push and moved over to the door. While I gripped the knob with one hand, I reached into my pocket and brought out the pack of book matches. As soon as I heard the buzzer answered, I swung the door open and stepped through. I turned and lodged the matches between the doorframe and the lock. I pushed the door shut and spun around.

The only light came from the second landing. It was enough to show me that the stairs were on the left. To the right there was a hall and a row of doors leading to apartments. Dark back there.

I started up the stairs. I was halfway up when a long shape, tall and narrow, blocked out part of the light by appearing on the landing. "Hardman? Frankie's up here."

"Coming."

I was four steps away from him when I heard the squeaking board in the dark hall below. It was reflex and the wrong move: I turned and looked back. That was when the tall man made his move. I felt rather than saw it. I pushed away from the railing toward the wall. Something hard hit the railing where I'd been a split second before. I bounced off the wall and grabbed at him. I got a handful of wet wool topcoat. I pulled the man in closer to me. At the same time I used my other hand to feel for what he'd swung at me. I caught the end of it and tried to hang on. It was a piece of pipe about a foot long. I had the untaped part of it and there were rough knurls, as if the pipe hadn't been sawed evenly. When the tall man pulled the pipe away from me, I had to let it go or tear up my palm.

I didn't let the whole edge go to him. As soon as I released the pipe, I balled the hand into a fist and dropped it low, a short chop aimed for his balls. He'd expected that and he swung his body away from me. The fist landed on the point of his hip. It jammed a couple of knuckles and I couldn't hold back a gasp of pain. That could have been the whole war, but the blow to his hip had hurt him some too and his breath pumped out at me, garlic and onions and tomatoes overpowering the cologne or aftershave he wore.

It was all happening fast and I couldn't forget the squeaking board below. Probably another man was coming up or setting himself to block any possible retreat. I knew I had to cover myself. I was still pulling him close, holding onto the damp topcoat, and he was trying to pull away. He wanted some distance so he could use the length of pipe. At the same time he was stomping for my feet and I was dancing. Then, suddenly, I used all my weight to swing him around. He was lower than me now, with his back to the bottom of the stairs. He was mad now, pulling away as hard as he could and I was pulling back with all my strength, until I released my hold on the topcoat and let him fall away. He lost his balance and stumbled down three or four steps before he caught the railing. He steadied himself and lifted the pipe.

"Now, you dumb shit," he said, "now I'm going to break your balls."

I backed up, feeling for the steps. Below him, another man moved into the light, a shorter man, broad and thick across the shoulders. Dark skin. Mex or Puerto Rican. Big hands up and out in front of him. No pipe. This one would depend on his strength.

Below, beyond them, a slight increase in the tempo of the rain and a cool chilled breeze. Hump came in fast and low, no sound, just a flash of movement. The short, broad one knew he was there first. He whirled around and Hump hit him twice. A right to the head and a left low to the body. The force of the blows threw that one into the tall one with the pipe, jostling him. The tall one divided his attention then, turning to his side and putting the pipe toward Hump. It was all I needed. I stepped down and swung a right deep into his kidney. It staggered him, buckling him at the knees. The pipe dropped out of his hand and clattered on the dark hall floor below. He grabbed the railing with both hands, trying to hold on until he could recover from the pain. I moved closer. Beyond him, Hump grabbed the short one and lifted him and turned him. He rammed him into the door. The glass part of the door shattered from the impact, showering the floor with fragments.

The tall one still couldn't move. A cripple and I didn't care. I leaned in and hit him in the same kidney. What came out of his mouth was part scream and part grunt. He held onto the railing with one hand and fell to his knees facing me. I think he would have begged if he could have brought the words up. I didn't give him time. I kicked him in the face and he went rolling down the steps toward Hump.

I watched him hit bottom and then I went up the steps to the second-floor landing. I turned right and moved down the hall. The door marked with a tarnished 8 was open. I went in. Empty. No furniture. A jar lid on the windowsill was full of cigarette butts. The window overlooked the street. So he'd been watching.

Hump waited for me at the bottom of the stairs. He nodded toward the one he'd broken up. "Shorty's out and not saying much." He stuck out a shoe and nudged the other one. "Tall Stuff's not talking either. Says he just got word a man with a lot of cash would be coming here. The call gave him the time and the whole setup with apartment 8. But he says he doesn't know who made the call."

"Who called you?" I leaned over him.

"Fuck off."

"Frankie call you? He set it up?"

He didn't say anything. I guess that could mean yes.

"Where's Frankie now?"

Tall Stuff lifted a hand toward me. Blood ran down his hand. He'd landed in the broken glass and made a mess of himself. I could see the bones and the tendons. He turned the palm toward him and looked at it and passed out.

Hump and I left him on the floor with the other stud and walked through the steady rain toward Sixth Avenue. Somewhere over there we'd find a bar where we could get a stiff drink.

"How?"

I didn't know. It was Thursday morning and we'd been in New York since Monday night. The night before, after we'd had the brawl at the apartment house on Eighth Avenue, I'd placed a call to Beth Fanzia. So far there'd been no new try on Edward. He was staying in the Towers, close to home, but I didn't think we could stay in New York much longer if we didn't find Frankie. It was expensive as hell, and a hard place to find anyone who didn't want to be found.

"I'm open to a suggestion," I said.

"One possibility," Hump said. "Tuesday morning you made the rounds and left notes for Frankie."

"Four places," I said.

"Maybe he doesn't use all those places anymore. Maybe he's down to only one of them."

"How do we find that out?"

"Easy. We backtrack and see if any of the messages weren't picked up. And we see which one was."

"Foxy," I said.

It was easy. The countermen at the two sandwich shops said they hadn't seen Frankie. I picked up the envelopes with the Tuesday messages in them and passed them each five. At the newsstand on Sixth Avenue it was the same. The old man there returned the note and admitted, when I passed him a five, that he hadn't seen Frankie for more than a month. That left the clam and oyster bar off Eighth Street. It was the only one left. It had to be the right one.

By noon, we'd set up shop in a cafe and bar across the street from the clam and oyster place. We'd bought ourselves the table near the front window. It cost us a ten and the promise of more to come. The waiter kept us in beer and the food wasn't bad, either. About two, I had the baked stuffed shrimp and Hump had a steak.

Even in the chill the place across the street was doing a good business. There were a few tables out in the open and the customers waited outside until the trays of opened oyster or clams were brought out to them. Then they'd shiver and throw their heads back, sucking the shellfish from the shells.

It was a long wait. It was getting to the fall darkness, the gray part of the day, when I saw Frankie strutting down the street, not a care in the world. He was dressed the same, blue jeans and a denim jacket. The way he approached the oyster bar, without precautions, I guessed he might be a little high. Or perhaps he'd called and found out that no one matching my description had been by.

After he entered, pushing his way past a couple of girls who were swallowing about a dozen oysters, I nodded at Hump. I dropped a twenty on the table and waved at the waiter. Outside the door, on the sidewalk, we split. Hump angled across the street. He headed toward a dark doorway we'd picked out earlier. It was in the direction from which Frankie had come. I went in the other direction. I'd cover the other end of the street. I backed into the doorway of a laundry and leaned against a scarred door frame.

Frankie came out after about ten minutes. He had an oyster shell in each hand and he stopped beside one of the tables and put a drop of Texas Pete on each oyster before he sucked them down one after the other. After he threw the shells into a barrel, he turned and walked down the street the way he'd come. He didn't look back. I left the doorway and headed after him. I'd made up some of the distance by the time he reached the doorway where Hump was. Hump was a blur coming out of the darkness. He wrapped an arm around Frankie's neck and pulled him into the doorway. I reached them in time to hear Frankie say, forcing it out against the hard ridge of forearm under his chin, "Take the money."

"Relax," I said.

Hump released Frankie and spun him around. He slammed against the door. "Be still," Hump said.

"Oh, it's you two. I've been looking all over town for you."

"Sure you have."

Frankie leaned toward Hump. Hump stiff-armed him and threw him against the door again. "I told you to be still."

"Why were you looking for us?" I edged over until I was shoulder to shoulder with Hump.

"I wanted you to know that it wasn't my fault last night."

"What?"

"Setting you up. Jim, they fooled me. They had me set up the meet with you and then they held me over in a room in the East Village so I couldn't warn you."

"Is that a fact?"

Hump nodded at me. "This pig is sweating."

"I guess we make him nervous." I patted Frankie on the shoulder. "We make you nervous, old friend?"

"It's not that. I thought you might not believe me."

"I believe you." I elbowed Hump. "We believe him, don't we?"

"All the way," Hump said. "If I didn't, I'd stomp him into pig shit."

"See? Hump and I thought you might have something to tell us."

"Huh?"

"What you had for us last night," I said.

"That? It was probably a pack of lies."

"We'll laugh in the right places."

"Like on cue," Hump said.

"That Count, whatever his name was, it wasn't him. It was somebody else."

"Who?"

"He didn't say."

"Who didn't say?"

I could smell the greasy sweat on him. "I can't tell you that."

"You more afraid of him than you are of us?"

"Hey," Frankie said, "I thought we were friends."

"Past tense," I said.

"Last night was not friendly," Hump said.

"All right." He dropped his voice to a whisper. "It wasn't anybody from New York or overseas. It was somebody from out west."

"Where?"

"Just out west. Some guy with a lot of money to spend."

I nudged Hump. "You believe him?"

"I'd like to talk to his asshole buddy, the one who helped set us up."

"I can't do that," Frankie said. "You'll be going back to Atlanta but I got to stay here and make a living. Or just keep living."

"He scare you or buy your ass?"

Frankie said, "Some of both."

"See what he's carrying, Hump."

Hump put his left hand on Frankie's throat. He held him upright while his other hand patted him down. He found the roll in the right front pocket of Frankie's jeans. He passed it back to me. I stepped out of the doorway so I'd have enough light to do a count by. Just a rough total put the sum up near seven hundred. I counted out my three hundred and pocketed it. I stepped back in the doorway and stuffed the rest of the roll into Frankie's shirt pocket.

"I took mine back," I said. "I don't think you ought to make a profit on me."

"What were we worth on the market?" Hump asked.

"Five hundred."

"Cheap for two people," Hump said. "What do you want to do with him, Jim?"

"Nothing. I don't want any marks on him. I think his other friends will be looking for him. If they aren't already. After what happened to Short Stuff and Tall Stuff, they're going to wonder if Frankie didn't turn right around and job them to us."

"That's neat enough for me." Hump dropped his hand and we backed out of the doorway. Frankie came after us. He caught me by the arm. "You really think they will? Come after me?"

"Sure. Right now they're thinking how bad the whole thing smells. I was supposed to be alone and I wasn't. And his rough boys got roughed."

"What do you think I ought to do, Hardman?"

"Sweat."

Later that night we flew back to Atlanta.

# CHAPTER NINE

After we got past the desk guard on the Templeton floor, Hump went looking for Edward. I'd put him up to it. I wanted him to keep Edward busy while I did some pushing and pulling at Beth. If I didn't find out what I wanted to know, there was still Edward. I'd rip some skin off him until I got the facts.

A breakfast cart was set up in the living room of Beth's suite. She was having a late breakfast: poached eggs on wheat toast and hot tea. I shook my head at the offer of a cup of tea from the pot and mixed myself a short drink of bourbon at the sideboard.

"Beth, I think you know who wants Edward dead. He's from out west and he's rich enough to spend any amount to get the killing done."

"I don't know any such thing."

"What do you know about Edward's life during the last thirty years?"

"Very little."

"I'll take what little you know."

"I can't tell you. It's too personal."

"So is being dead." I looked down at the drink. "I know that Edward deserted the navy back in 1943."

"It wasn't that way at all." There was fire and anger in her now. It flared out at me.

"Tell me how it was."

"Edward did that for me. That's all I can tell you."

"It's not enough. Look, dammit, whoever wants Edward dead wants it done if it takes another year. Or five years. We can hire an army and buy us some automatic weapons and we can turn this floor into a stockade. And it still might not be enough."

"What you said, a rich man out west. I hadn't thought about that in years. I swear I haven't."

"What was it about?"

"It's hard to tell you. Especially you."

"Shit, Beth, you want to wait until Edward's dead and buried? You want to wait until you've ordered the stone? 'Beloved Brother,' that kind of shit."

"You can be rough, Jim."

"Tell me about it." I knew my face was hard, knowing I wouldn't get what I wanted unless it was.

"I was fourteen and Daddy was busy in Washington. It was the second year of the war and it wasn't going well. Daddy was a dollar-a-year man."

I nodded. While I listened, I was doing some figuring in my head. Fourteen in 1943. That meant she was two or three years older than I was.

"So Daddy sent me out to stay with an old friend and his family out in Oklahoma City."

The strain was on her. It broke the smooth skin and put the lines and wrinkles where they were supposed to be.

The friend was a man her father's age, in oil. Big in oil. His wife was a sweet woman, a kind woman. And there was a daughter, Francine, who was about Beth's age. But the man had a male ruttiness to him and Beth didn't really know what sex was. It was an innocent time then and what a girl knew, she had heard from girls her own age, or she got from those Hollywood movies of the time.

Beth found in that man the kind of father she'd never known in old Rufus Templeton. It had been beautiful and warm until one night when all the fun and tenderness changed and he'd hurt her and hurt her and hurt her and when it was over she wasn't a virgin anymore and she knew what sex was. For a few nights after that, he visited her late when his wife and daughter were asleep and he'd taken the last shreds of her maidenhead, until she forced him away by threatening to tell his wife and daughter. After that, he stayed at a distance. But by then the damage had been done. Within two months she knew she was pregnant and she didn't know what to do about it. She couldn't talk to the man's wife or daughter and she couldn't talk to him.

What she settled upon was done in desperate shock. She told the family she was going to San Diego to see her brother Edward before he shipped out. She drew all her money out of the bank and caught a bus. Edward was supposed to be at the destroyer base. When she reached San Diego, she found that he'd left, shipped north to Treasure Island, the naval station in the bay between Oakland and San Francisco. She followed him there by train. In time she found him and though it was hard, she blurted it out to him. He was in a violent rage for almost an hour. Then he calmed down and started checking around. Finally he found an officer who knew about a doctor who'd perform the abortion for a thousand dollars. Time was running out. He was on the ready list.

The abortion was done. Still, it was not an easy time for her. He couldn't leave her alone in the city. He had to stay with her until he was sure there were no complications. It was a week before he was sure she was past the worst of it. By then his ship had left and he was A.W.O.L.

When she asked what he was going to do, he wouldn't say. He said he'd figure out something. He'd placed a call for her to Washington and she'd said she didn't want to go back to Oklahoma City, lying and saying she didn't get along with the daughter, and her father had been angry but he had arranged for a seat for her on a train heading back east, back to Atlanta. On that train she'd cried almost all the first night. The memory that she carried for years was before her, of Edward standing alone on the platform of the Oakland train station, waving at her and trying to smile, knowing he was in trouble, and that he couldn't tell the real reason why he'd missed his ship. And even if he could, not knowing if it was a reason the navy would accept.

And that was the last time she'd seen him until he'd appeared in Atlanta a few weeks before.

"Who was the man in Oklahoma City?"

"Alec Troutman."

"Him?" I'd heard of him. He was still one of the big names in oil. Just before the war he'd hit one of the big oil fields in Texas and after the war he'd branched out into Arabian oil. I had seen an article on him a few months back that put his wealth at nearly five hundred million and still growing. I remembered a picture of him too, one that had been in *Time* or *Newsweek*. He was around eighty-five now, his face dark and angry-looking. But he'd aged well and he didn't look much past fifty.

"Did you see Troutman … after that?"

"No. I didn't have to. He and Daddy had a falling out over some off-shore leases and they didn't see each other after that."

"Your father never knew?"

"You're the first person I've ever told."

I carried my drink over to the sideboard and put the glass on a tray. "Why now? If Troutman wanted to hurt somebody, why would he wait until now? And why Edward? Why not you?"

"I can't answer that."

"Maybe Edward can," I said.

"I don't want you to talk to him, Jim. Please don't."

"I'm sorry, Beth. I really am. The thing is, I need to know if there's some connection between Edward and Troutman."

"I think you want me to hate you."

"No." I moved over to her and tipped her face back. There was a misting of tears in her eyes. I kissed her on the mouth, tasting her salt or mine. Gentle. Oh, that was a gentle and kindly kiss.

❧ ❧ ❧

The door to Edward's bedroom was closed and locked. I rapped on it a couple of times and Hump opened it. There was smoke in the air and the smell of the kind of wood-burn that a dull saw makes. Hash.

Hump waved me in. "Edward's got some A-1 hash. We've been giving it a tryout."

"How is it?" I stepped through the doorway and Hump closed the door and locked it behind me.

"It's like beating yourself with a big stick," Hump said.

Edward was stretched out on the bed, with the hash pipe in the cup of his hand. I scooped up a chair on the way to the bed and plopped it down where I could face him. "I've been talking to Beth."

Edward grinned, sleepy, loose. "You two have been doing a lot of that lately. Can I assume your intentions are honorable?"

Behind me, Hump laughed.

"Not me. I can't afford to play the course." I got out a smoke and lit it. "This time we've been talking about when she was fourteen and staying with Alec Troutman and his family in Oklahoma."

"That was a long time ago." Edward closed his eyes. "You can't expect me to remember everything that happened thirty years ago."

"After Beth came to see you in San Francisco…"

Edward sat up and swung his legs over the side of the bed. He looked past me. "Hump, you do me a favor?"

"Sure."

"Find your way out to the kitchen and get us a round of beer. And…take your time. I think your friend Hardman and I have something to talk about in private."

"Fifteen minutes enough?"

"I think so," Edward said.

Hump looked at his watch and went out and closed the door behind him. Edward watched him go. Then he put the hash pipe on the night table and leaned over to hook my pack of smokes with a couple of fingers. "How much did Beth tell you?"

"All of it. Up to the time you put her on a train in Oakland."

"You think it's worth it, raking all this up again?"

"I wouldn't do it otherwise." I got out a book of matches and lit his cigarette. "After you saw Beth off, what did you do?"

"I caught a bus to Oklahoma City."

"To see Troutman?"

He nodded. He got there early in the afternoon and he waited out front until Alec Troutman arrived. It was about dusk when he faced Troutman and told him he knew about what had happened to Beth. Troutman had cried then, and he'd tried to explain. Edward hadn't listened to any of it. He'd beaten Troutman to the ground and he'd straddled him and kept hitting him until Troutman passed out, still crying and still trying to explain. Edward broke his nose, shattered one cheekbone and might have killed him if he hadn't broken a hand.

"And then?"

He rode the bus all night to Dallas, the broken hand swelling in his lap. As soon as he arrived, he called Beth in Atlanta and later that day Beth wired him all the money she could collect or borrow in such a short time. He found a doctor who fixed the broken hand and he took a room in a boarding house. He stayed there for a month while the hand healed. During this time he established a new identity for himself, a social security card in the name of Edward Temple. And he'd gone to the rackets for a draft card. Only the card he bought, instead of giving his status as 4F, rated him as 1A and moved his age back a couple of years.

When the hand was healed, he went to the navy recruiting office and enlisted. He spent the next three years, after boot camp and aviation electrician school, on a jeep carrier ferrying aircraft out to the Pacific. He made third class petty officer and he was honorably discharged in 1946.

"I didn't work long at any job: a year here, a year there."

"Why?"

"Somebody found me. I don't know how long they'd been looking. One night in 1947, outside a bar in Alameda, a man tried to run me down in a parking lot."

"Troutman?"

"I don't know. I thought it might be. I moved to Chicago. After a couple of years there, I decided it might be easier to lose myself in small towns. And each place I got so I could feel it. I'd know they'd found me and I'd leave town. It was a year here, six months in the next town. And then I thought I'd lost them for good. The last five years I was in a commune in Arizona."

"Disguised as a hippie?"

"No. To tell the truth, I believed in that kind of life, in the better parts of it." He lifted the pipe and set it in his teeth. From a piece of foil on the night table he broke off a chip of hash. "You mind?"

I shook my head.

"Had to be sure." He got the chip sizzling in the pipe. The wood-burn smell was harsh when it reached me. "I got so I believed that it didn't matter how successful you were, or how unsuccessful. The real thing was to get by, to live a good life. That the millionaire and the hippie, when they're dead, rot and stink in about the same way."

"And then you heard your father was dying?"

He nodded. "And as soon as I arrived here, it started again."

I stood up. "You could have saved us a lot of trouble if you'd told me this before."

"Beth deserved it, all the silence." He drew the smoke in and held it. "You see, she's had a hard life. Those husbands, those divorces, probably have their roots back in what Troutman did to her back when she was a kid. It's not really all her fault."

"Maybe."

"It might be a good sign, the fact that she could talk to you about it."

"Call me Dr. Hardman," I said.

A couple of minutes later Hump brought in three cold Buds.

Back a couple of years ago, a newspaper and magazine writer, a guy who did some financial writing on a freelance basis, split with his wife. She wanted a divorce and about all he owned. Hump and I did the dirty work for him, working on the assumption that no woman wants a divorce until she's picked out her next husband. We'd been wrong about that. But not altogether wrong about her. For several days we watched her and she looked straight until Hump remarked that he thought her lawn was getting more work than it really needed. So we started paying attention to the seventeen-year-old boy who did her yard work. We noticed that he spent quite a bit of time in the house and several times when he left his hair was damp, as if he'd just had a shower. He was a good-looking kid, a senior in high school, and a jock. It didn't take much to frighten the kid into making a statement about his affair with the wife. There'd been a lot of afternoon bush-shaking going on.

Faced with the statement, the wife settled for a new home, a car, and a lump settlement. And it had been a very small lump compared to what she'd wanted in the first place. And all of this meant that Arvin Cross, the writer, owed me a favor.

The house we'd helped him keep is in one of the older sections of town, Ansley Park, and it was once a lawyer's home. In those days some lawyers did their business at home. If the lawyer really wanted to be fancy, he'd build him a small, separate building on the property that served as an office. The man who'd built Cross's home back around the turn of the century had been that kind of lawyer. Now Cross used the little cottage as a workroom.

"Alec Troutman? What about him?"

His face was hawkish and lean. He took off his wire-rimmed glasses and placed them on the cluttered desk. He blinked at me and the pink, tired eyes reminded me of a white mouse.

"How well do you know him?"

"I talked to him half a day once when I was doing a piece on him about five years ago."

"A sympathetic piece?"

"He liked it," Cross said.

"I need to know where he is. And if it can be arranged, I'd like to talk to him."

"That won't be easy. Oh, I think I can find out where he is. The odds are that he won't see you."

"Say I'm a writer who wants to do a piece on him."

Cross shook his head. "You wouldn't get past the check he'd have done on you."

"Find him then."

It took two long-distance calls. One to the east coast office in New York and another, after clearance there, to the main office in Dallas. After some rambling talk about oil depletion and off-shore drilling and the need for a new look at the oil industry, Cross had the information. He put the receiver back in its cradle and grinned at me. "You won't believe this, but Troutman is right here in Atlanta."

I believed it. Why not? He wanted Edward Templeton dead and after thirty years of wanting it, maybe he'd decided to be close enough to smell the blood when it happened. "Where?"

"It seems there's no chance of doing another article about him. He's pretty sick. If I read between the lines, what they were telling me was that he might even be dying."

"Where?"

"The Dansler Clinic. It's over near Georgia Tech."

I nodded. I'd heard something about it years ago, but I couldn't remember exactly what had been said.

"It's the rich man's last hope. That and a dieting clinic for rich fat kids. Something like the rice diet up at Duke."

"What's Troutman doing out there?"

"They didn't say. I'll tell you this. The time I saw him there wasn't a spare ounce on him."

"So what's the clinic specialty?"

"Miracles," Cross said.

"Can I get in?"

"The clinic?" He looked me up and down. "Sure. Find yourself a doctor who'll refer you. You could stand to lose thirty pounds."

I gave him the high finger and went looking for a doctor. It wasn't hard to find a gullible one. Doctors, though they don't like to admit it, are just as bright or just as stupid as anybody else. So I just shopped around until I found one who'd probably cheated to pass most of his exams.

The main clinic building was like the mansion on some old pre-war plantation. That is, except for the glitter of wire strands and broken glass at the top of the nine-foot stone walls and the gate with the guards on duty twenty-four hours a day. Not that it looked like a maximum-security slammer. The precautions, I guess they'd say, were for their famous guests who didn't want to be bothered. And they'd have mentioned a talk show host, a novelist whose last book had been on the *Times* list for more than twenty weeks and an actress who specialized in playing kindly but misguided mothers. All of these were people the news media had a tendency to badger if they could.

Past the gate there were long green lawns with brick paths reaching out in all directions. These were the exercise paths, for the walking and jogging the clinic recommended.

Scattered beyond the main clinic building, in a wooded area, were the cottages, units with a living room, a bedroom, and a bath. There were larger units with a spare bedroom and a kitchen.

The doctor who'd referred me to the clinic had been careful to let me know that these cottages were somewhat expensive. Many of the people in for the diet lived in the wards. And he'd given me a booklet which boasted about the fact that several of the larger units had up-to-date hospital equipment, that twenty-four-hour-a-day nursing service was available, and that doctors and residents were on call at all hours.

Money wouldn't be a problem for Alec Troutman. He'd be in the best cottage. I was sure of that.

Hump drove me out to the clinic. He remained in the waiting room. To maintain the image of a faithful employee, he'd dressed in a plain black suit and a ratty tie and he'd carried my suitcase for me.

I didn't see Dr. Dansler right away. First, I had to undress down to my shorts and undergo a medical examination: heart and blood pressure and cough and a slow kneading of the fat roll around my waist. And while I dressed, the questions about my eating and drinking habits. On one page headed DIET PROFILE, I had to give him a detailed account of what I'd eaten for breakfast, lunch, and dinner the day before. I was careful to add a few fats and starches: hash browns and buttered toast for breakfast, at lunch french fries and buttered rolls, and for supper a baked potato with butter and sour cream and a wedge of Boston cream pie.

The young doctor shook his head sadly a few times, as if he'd heard this foolishness a number of times before. And I stayed in my role by thinking that he probably had one of those special metabolisms that allowed gluttony without punishing him for it.

The diet profile completed and all my clothing back on, he walked me down a bright hallway to the inner office. I waited outside while he carried my medical exam sheet and diet profile in to the great man. I guess they were talking my case over but I couldn't hear anything they said about me.

After about five minutes the young doctor bowed me into the office. I sat across the desk from Dr. Dansler and looked him over while he did his estimate of me. He was a man of about sixty, spare and lean. A tan covered a mass of facial wrinkles. Pale gray eyes, accented by neat silver hair, peered at me, reading my body even with clothing on it, and putting price tags on my suit, the shirt, the tie, and the shoes.

"You don't seem quite as overweight as our usual guest, Mr. Hardman."

I told him I thought I'd better do something about it before it really got out of hand. Anyway, I said, I'd read somewhere that even one pound overweight was a bad strain on the heart.

"Of course. Quite right." He stared down at my shiny new file for a minute or so. "According to Dr. Black, you appear to be about twenty-five pounds overweight."

I nodded and I hoped looked properly humble about it.

"Two weeks at a controlled diet with supervised exercise and you should be in tiptop condition." He closed the file. "Of course you could carry out the same kind of program for yourself."

I said I didn't think I had the will power to do it alone.

I think he'd heard that before, many times. He stood up and shook my hand and gave me directions to the business office. Ten minutes later I'd written a check for $1400, payment in advance for the first week's stay. It could have been less, but I decided to take one of the smaller cottages. I needed the freedom of movement the privacy would give me. Sooner or later I'd have to look for Alec Troutman so we could have a talk.

The deposit, I was told, was not returnable if I left the diet program without Dr. Dansler's approval.

A huge black bruiser of an orderly carried my suitcase and led Hump and me to cottage number 8. He unlocked the door, placed the suitcase on a chair and opened it.

"You don't have to do that," I said.

"Afraid I do, sir," he said. "You'd be surprised the kinds of food people smuggle in. Cakes, cookies, and even cans of beans."

"Nothing in there," I said, "but help yourself." I'd expected some kind of search so I hadn't packed a piece. Hump had brought it in for me. When the orderly's back was to me I nodded at the bathroom. Hump went in and closed the door. A minute later the john flushed and he came out. Passing me he whispered, "In the towels."

When the unpacking was done, Hump and the orderly left. I sat down on the bed and waited for lunch. It wasn't worth waiting for. On the tray there was a glass of some kind of juice, a bowl of rice, and a small dish of sliced peaches.

After lunch, the orderly came for me and we walked on the exercise paths for half an hour before he took me to the gym, where I was outfitted in a heavy sweatsuit and tennis shoes and turned over to a drill inspector type who bullied about twenty of us fat men into a kind of scared sweat. First came exercises and then volleyball until I could hardly stand up. I sat down in the shower and drank cold water straight from the shower nozzle.

I took a nap until six. Supper was some kind of drink like Tang and another bowl of rice and a dish of mandarin orange slices. And a small pot of coffee without sugar or cream.

It was slow time until it was full dark. Then I put on my heavy walking jacket and dug around in the towel rack until I found my .38 P.P. I stuffed it in my coat pocket and walked over to the recreation room in the main building.

I drank a cup of mint tea and watched some sloppy ping-pong games. Fat people don't move that well and there was an especially awkward game of mixed doubles. I took my time. I was looking for a mark, a talkative type. Someone with the loose, hanging flesh that meant they'd been at the clinic for a time.

I found him at last. He came in while I was having a second cup of the tea: a man about forty who was wearing a pair of slacks about four inches too big for him. And a shirt that could wrap around him.

He moved over to the magazine section. He got a copy of *Time*. I got *Sports Illustrated* and sat down near him. I was skimming an article on the Dolphins when I looked up and saw him staring at me.

"New here, huh?"

"First day," I said, "and I'm starving."

"You get used to it. A week and you almost get to like the rice and the fruit."

So that was his approach. He was the old salt, the veteran, and he'd talk and talk and talk to the rookie. All I had to do was go along with the conversation and not seem to control it. In time I'd know all he knew. It wasn't hard. He wanted to know if I was in the ward or one of the cottages. The fact that I'd taken the cottage gave me a kind of status. He said he was in the ward because he liked to be close to people.

I nodded as if I believed him and he was off and running.

Within a few minutes I knew all about the famous guests who'd visited the clinic during his time. It wasn't far from there to gossip about the mysterious patient, the one in deluxe cottage number 1. There was always a large black Continental parked in front, though the other guests had to store their cars in the clinic lot. And once he'd passed by the cottage when the telephone company truck was outside and he'd seen three telephones taken inside. Hard-looking men were coming and going at all hours. One of the diet patients, a big reader of mystery novels, believed that the man in deluxe cottage number 1 was a famous Mafia figure who was in hiding from the F.B.I.

It was cool and dark outside, with an overcast sky. Clouds that would cover me, I hoped. When I knew enough, I fought back a yawn and said the starving and the exercise had tired me. Old salt to the last, he'd said in no time I'd feel like a new man, like he did.

Now I blundered from cottage to cottage. Over half of them were dark, no lights showing, and I knew the dead-out ones were rice-diet people like me, starved into a kind of hopeless submission.

As soon as I saw the dark outline of the Continental, I knew I'd found the right one. Lights burned on the right side of the cottage and I moved in that direction. I came from the rear, taking a long loop to get there, and I used the shadow cover to reach the first lighted window. A bathroom. No one there. I pressed against the wall and edged toward the next window. The blinds were down but cracked slightly. At first, I wasn't sure what I saw. It seemed to be some kind of white-on-white modern painting. And then the nurse who'd been leaning over the bed with her back to me straightened up and stepped aside.

No doubt about it. It was Alec Troutman. The lean angry face I'd seen in the magazines now puffy, swollen. His mouth was open, lips quivering, as he gasped for air. While I watched, the nurse approached the bed from the other side. She reached out a hand and dropped a pill or tablet of some kind into Troutman's mouth. It reminded me of the way I'd seen a sick cat given medicine once. The nurse put her hand on Troutman's chin, forced his mouth closed and held it that way until the old man swallowed.

Not a good time to talk to him. Perhaps tomorrow.

I edged away from the wall. I was fifty yards away from the cottage, circling away, when I heard the click. It was a hammer going back on cock. I'd heard it enough in my time. Hear it a few times and you don't forget.

Right away, knowing I didn't have much time, I dropped into a deep knee bend and I did a few more before the flashlight glare hit me full in the face.

I stopped in the squat and said, "What … what are you … ?"

"Who are you?" The light was steady on me.

"I'm Harper, Jim Harper. I'm at the diet clinic."

"What are you doing out here?"

"Walking and exercising. I'm supposed to …"

The front door to the cottage opened. A man moved from the doorway, the light framing him. "Something going on, Artie?"

"Some guy doing exercises, Mr. Clark."

"This time of night?" He was a tall, narrow man, with sloping shoulders and a long, flat loaf of a face, dark hair and pale skin above a dark robe. "Is he fat?"

"Yeah, Mr. Clark."

"Point him in another direction," Clark said. "Tell him to do his squats somewhere else." He closed the door and the light wagged across me.

"You heard the man."

I straightened up and walked away. After a few feet the light went out. Then I could reach up and run a hand over my face. The sweat on it felt chilled, like the condensation on the sides of a tall drink.

During the night I dreamed about a thick slice of prime rib. It seemed to be about a foot thick and the blood running down the sides of it bubbled and hissed.

Rice and purple plums and carrot juice. Hot black tea in the small pot. I was pouring the tea down the john when the orderly came for me. After a few minutes of walking he turned me back toward the gym. There, in a sweatsuit and tennis shoes, the D.I. type ran us through straddle-jumps and deep knee bends. When the rasp of breathing got up to heart attack level, he paired us off and we tossed a medicine ball back and forth for half an hour. I might not have lasted if the fat man with me hadn't kept dropping the ball on his foot.

Showered and dressed, I left the gym and traced my path from the night before. I reached the place where I'd been stopped. Then I realized something had happened. I could see the black Continental parked a few yards from the front door to the cottage. What was new was the ambulance there, the rear doors open. While I kept my distance and watched, two attendants wheeled out a stretcher bed. A blanket-covered body was on the bed. They lifted the stretcher and rammed the bed through the back of the ambulance and slammed the doors shut.

Dr. Black, the young one who'd given me the examination the day before, stood on the lawn in front of the cottage and shook his head as the ambulance pulled away and headed in the direction of the front gate. Still shaking his head, he walked toward me. He saw me and stopped. "Mr. Hardman … right?"

I nodded. "What happened?"

"A death," he said.

"Anybody I know?"

"You might have heard of him," Dr. Black said. "A Mr. Alec Troutman."

"I've heard of him. Natural causes?"

"Of course." He looked shocked that I'd think otherwise. He seemed to regret that he'd spoken to me at all. He gave me a tight, grim nod and walked away.

I might have turned away if the Continental hadn't been parked there. It made me think someone might still be in the cottage. I walked across the lawn and knocked at the door.

After a few seconds, the door was opened a foot or so. The man beyond the door was the one who'd stood there last night, the one in the robe who'd been called Mr. Clark. The way he stared at me, I was fairly certain he didn't remember me. "What do you want?"

"I'm Jim Hardman."

"Hardman?" His eyes raked over me, seeing me for the first time. "Am I supposed to know you?"

"I'd like to talk to you."

"For what good it'll do, come on in." He hit the door with the heel of his hand and swung it open. I followed him inside. We were in a living room. Dark red leather furniture, with the smell of the leather or whatever they cleaned it with strong around us. "Am I supposed to know who you are?"

"I work for the Templetons."

His face didn't show it but I felt he knew who I was. "You heard about Mr. Troutman?"

"I heard."

"Then what do you want with me?"

"Now that Troutman's dead, does that end it?"

"End what?"

"Come on," I said. "I've got it worked out. That's why I'm here."

He looked at my waistline and grinned. "I thought it was for the rice."

I walked past him and looked into the bedroom. The sheets were stripped from the bed, balled up on the floor, waiting for some orderly to remove the death signs. "I don't know who you are."

"I'm Frank Clark. I was Mr. Troutman's executive assistant."

"You ought to be able to answer my question. Is it over?"

"What?"

"The try on Templeton."

"On poor Edward?" He dropped into one of the leather easy chairs, put his head back, and laughed.

I let it run down until it was somewhere between a sob and a giggle. I said, "Let me in on the joke and I'll laugh with you."

"You won't," he said.

"Try me."

"See if you can laugh about this. Yesterday, when the old man finally realized he was dying, that he didn't have much time left, he made the big deal. It's the one that assured him that he would get what he wanted more than anything else in the world.

"What was that?"

"Revenge. Satisfaction against a man who'd stomped him into the dirt like a bug."

"How?"

"He bought himself a death squad."

"Go on."

"He paid in cash. One hundred thousand dollars. It's a non-revocable contract. It's to be carried out no matter what happens to him."

"Tell me about it," I said.

"Fuck you, Hardman," he said, all the laughter gone. "Fuck you and Templeton."

"Nothing can stop it?"

"You can quit," he said.

He wouldn't say anything more. I left him and went to my cottage and packed my suitcase. I called Hump from a phone in the main building. He picked me up at the main gate about half an hour later.

# CHAPTER TEN

"A death squad?"

I was having my second big meal since I'd been rescued from the rice and fruit. For lunch, I'd had two Big Macs and a vanilla shake on the way back into town.

Now, for dinner, Hump and Art Maloney and I were at the Butcher Block, a steak house on Luckie. I'd ordered myself about a two-inch sirloin and a big potato with butter and sour cream and I was planning on about a whole apple pie with my coffee.

Art had asked the question. I'd thought he might have an answer for me. That was why I'd invited him to dinner. But he'd answered my question about death squads with another question and that wasn't much help.

"That's what the man said."

"I'll ask."

"When?"

"Oh, shit," Art said. "You buy me the best steak I've seen in five years and now you want me to walk away from it and let it get cold." He stuffed a bloody wedge into his mouth.

"Time's short."

"It always is." He gave the rest of his steak a sad look and pushed back his chair. He went to the pay phone back by the rest room. He dialed one number and talked for a minute and then hung up and dialed another number. Again he talked for about a minute. On the way back to the table, he stopped off and spoke to the waiter. He sat down at the table, pulled his plate toward him, and cut another wedge. After he chewed it, he said, "It's still warm."

"I had Hump breathe on it."

"Thanks, Hump." He swallowed and looked over at me. "I talked to Intelligence. Nothing. Then I talked to the district F.B.I. agent and he said he'd check around and call me back."

"He know anything?"

"Seemed vague to me."

We were on coffee and Benedictine when the phone rang at the bar. The waiter waved a hand at Art and he went over and took the call at the pay phone. He talked for a couple of minutes, listening most of the time. Back at the table he shook his head. "Mostly rumors."

"I'll take rumors."

"Washington says it might be a new concept in killing for hire. You want Joe Blow offed, you need a gun and a wheelman. That could be pickup help. But say you want somebody done who's got good security. A big money man or a political figure or a labor leader. Then you've got to have more than casual help. You need a team that works together."

"How big a team?"

"They've heard stories about four-man squads. Kill anybody if the money is right. Specialists in weapons and explosives."

"What's new about that?" Hump asked.

"They train as a team. They work as a team. It's not pickup. It's forever."

I drained my coffee. I didn't feel too good. "Does steak curdle on your stomach?"

"It does on mine," Hump said.

"You still in?" I asked him.

"Might as well."

"You still got that Austrian shotgun?"

"Just like new," Hump said.

"We leave here, you go by and pick it up. On the way to my house stop by some pawn shop or K-Mart and pick up a hundred or so shells."

Art leaned in. "You two starting a war?"

"Maybe."

Hump asked, "Where'll you be?"

"Recruiting."

I was in the back booth of the Gray Horse Tavern out on Ponce de Leon. The man across from me had been a cop back in the early sixties and he'd been wiped off the force because he'd been too close to some gamblers and pimps. I wouldn't trust him with a five-dollar bill but he'd also been a hardass in his time. Tough and hard and go-to-hell, that was him. In the years since I'd last seen him, he'd done security for some department store or other. That was just a cover. He also ran some book. He looked out of shape now. He'd had trouble getting his belly into the booth.

"The money's good," I said.

"My burial insurance is already paid up."

Sad. He'd been a good man in his time, good with a rifle, hell with a handgun.

"You're saying no?"

He nodded.

"You know anybody?"

"I can call around. It would have to be somebody crazy."

"Make the calls," I said.

He was in the closed phone booth three or four minutes. I saw him make four or five calls, maybe more than that. When he came back, he stood out in the aisle. He lifted his drink. He wouldn't meet my eyes. "I made the calls."

"Thanks."

"If you don't mind, I've got business at the bar."

"Sure," I said.

"The word's out. Anybody interested will be here in the next hour."

"Appreciate it, Ed."

"Look." He leaned over me so his voice wouldn't carry as far as the bar. "I can't do that kind of stuff anymore. It all ran out of a hole in my toe."

I patted his shoulder. "You didn't say that. If you said it, I didn't hear you."

He sat for the next hour at the bar with his back to me. I couldn't tell if I'd made a friend or an enemy out of him.

Three men showed up. I culled the first one right away. It was that obvious. The bottle had him. And he didn't have much pride left: the white shirt he wore was so dirty he'd tried to talcum the collar and the cuffs. His hand trembled when he tried to lift the drink I bought him.

"I can't use you," I said. I palmed a five and slid it across the table toward him.

He lost half the drink, spilling it down his shirt, trying to get it down. He didn't thank me for the five.

The second one looked better. Young, about twenty-four or five. Good clothes but a bit on the loud side. Talked well about a year and a half in Nam. Had hunted all his life. Worked now as a bouncer in a downtown girl show. I was about to take him on, but first I went up to the bar to get myself another drink. The open space was next to Ed. When I pushed in there, he said, without turning to me, "The needle."

I carried my drink back to the booth. I put down the drink and said, "Roll up both sleeves."

"It's just skin-popping."

"Let me see the veins."

He slid out of the booth and walked outside without looking back at me.

The third one was just mouth. He'd seen too many cowboy movies or something. As soon as he sat down. he opened his jacket so I could see the butt of the chipped-handled .32. "I'm not afraid of anybody," he said.

"You do service time?"

"No."

"Police work?"

"No."

"Hunt much?"

He shook his head.

I shook my head back at him. "Maybe I can use you for a later job," I said, "but not this one."

He swaggered out. Probably scared to death and glad I couldn't use him.

The hour was up. I edged up on Ed at the bar. "A drunk, a needle, and a cowboy. It doesn't look good."

"The scared word is out. You can get fifty to knock over a supermarket. But not this one."

I thanked him and bought a round for the seven or eight men at the bar.

I was out in the parking lot when he called me from the doorway. "Where'll you be?"

"My place."

"How long?"

I looked at my watch. "Two hours."

"Anybody else comes by I'll call you."

"Cull them for me."

He nodded and waved.

I drove home. Hump was parked in the driveway waiting for me.

Hump put the wrapped weapon on the kitchen table and nodded at it. "Art dropped this by. He said you might find a use for it."

I untied the cords and unrolled the canvas. It was an Ml carbine, the officer's model, with a tube clip taped to each side of the
stock.

"I guess I can."

I guess you never forget. I field-stripped the carbine while
Hump sat across the table and drank a beer. It was in good shape,
no rust or pits.

I was in the bathroom washing the oil off my hands when the
phone rang. It was Ed at the Gray Horse Tavern.

"I think I've got you one."

"He look good?" My hands were dripping and I couldn't find
a towel in the bedroom. I dried my hands on the sheet.

"He might be the real thing."

"You know him?"

"No."

I asked what the guy called himself.

"Runt."

"Huh?"

"He's a cocky little bastard. You want to talk to him?"

"Send him out."

"Sure."

"And Ed?"

"Yeah?"

"Check around on him. See if anybody knows anything
about him."

He said he would. He'd call me back if he found out anything
I ought to know.

He came in as if he was about a foot taller than he really was. He
was a shade under five feet even with the heels on those scuffed
cowboy boots. Young, not more than twenty-three or twenty-
four. Hair blond and long, shaggy. Wearing tan jeans and a

fringed buckskin jacket. His face still had a few patches of acne and a couple of festering pimples down low on the side of one nostril.

"If you're the one hiring, I'm your man."

I waved him through the doorway and back toward the kitchen. I followed him in and watched while he and Hump looked each other up and down. He looked back over his shoulder. "This your whole army?"

"So far."

"You need help then." The Ml carbine leaned against the door where I'd left it. He jerked it up to inspection arms and cleared it. "You can't kill shit with this."

"Maybe you can't," I said.

He snapped it dry and leaned it back against the door frame.

I tapped the back of one of the chairs. "Sit down and tell me about yourself."

Hump opened the refrigerator and got out three Buds.

"How do you want it?"

"Name?"

"Bob Ward. They call me Runt."

"Tell me the rest of it."

He'd enlisted in the army at sixteen, using his older brother's birth certificate. Did a tour in Nam up on the line. Wounded about the time his tour was up. Back in the states for his eighteenth birthday. Discharged when they found out about the fraudulent enlistment. After that he'd worked for a year in one of the New Haven gun plants, test-firing M-16's. Recruited there by white African mercenaries. Fought there, in one country or another for three years. Good money. Ran out of jobs and came back to the states. Had thought about going back in the army, but they'd found out about the three years in Africa and wouldn't touch him. Now he was running out of cash and needed a job. He was expert with most arms. Pistol, rifle, or most automatic weapons. And he had some knowledge of plastic explosives.

"How'd you hear about the job?"

"Overheard some dude at a bar where I was having a drink. Bought him one and he pointed me to the Gray Horse Tavern." He poured about a third of the bottle into the back of his throat and burped. "This job. They're real pros?"

"From what I heard. Might be three or four of them."

"And against them," he said, "you've got you and big stud there?"

"That's right. And maybe you if you want in."

"Arms?"

"Anything you want. Anything we can find and buy."

He gave me the hard look. "You know which end the lead comes out of?"

I nodded.

"And Hump there?"

"He shot a tree once with a shotgun."

He threw his head back and laughed. "Lordy, lordy."

"You in?"

"Sure. I like lost causes."

"It might be the wrong job for you then. This might not be one."

"Why?"

"We pick the ground. We don't let them pick it."

"Where?"

"I have a place in mind."

"When?"

"We leave tonight. You need weapons?"

"I've got mine," he said.

"We didn't talk money."

"We'll negotiate after you see how much I'm worth."

At three a.m. an ambulance tore through traffic, siren going, and pulled up in front of the main entrance to the Melton Towers. Less than ten minutes later, accompanied by a frightened and crying old woman, the attendants wheeled out a stretcher bed and loaded it in the ambulance. The old woman got in back with one of the attendants and the driver threw rubber heading back toward town. A block away from Grady Hospital the ambulance cut the siren. It circled the hospital, passing up the emergency entrance and stopped on the street where Hump and I stood beside my car.

Edward got out and stepped into the car. I paid off the ambulance in cash and put a hundred on the old lady. She was Equity but I don't think she'd put this job down on her résumé the next time she went for an actor's cattle call.

A few blocks away, at the bus station, we picked up Runt. He was standing on the corner, one foot up on a gun-metal gray foot locker.

It took two of us to lift the foot locker and pack it away in the trunk of the car. As soon as it was loaded in, you could feel the tail drag.

# CHAPTER ELEVEN

By six a.m., we were far into the Georgia mountains. The air was clear now, after the cities were behind us. And it was cool, chilly as we felt the gradual incline in front of us. The headlights revealed that the leaves hadn't turned completely yet. It was still a matter of a week or two. After that it would be all flame and gold.

A few minutes after six, we passed through Harper Falls. It was a two-block town. All the fires were banked away until the sun warmed the street: not even a cafe or a restaurant open yet.

I drove it from memory. I'd been the route a few times before. Back a few years ago, a man I'd known in Atlanta had dropped out of city life. He and his wife had bought a piece of property just outside of Harper Falls. They'd brought their son with them and they'd had a cabin built on the side of a mountain. They got into mountain crafts, he into pottery and she into weaving, and they'd made it for a couple of years until the marriage went bad. His wife took the boy and moved to Macon and he'd stayed at the cabin another year. It hadn't been the same without the wife and the boy and he'd moved back to Atlanta and got back into advertising. Since then, he used the cabin a few times each summer and he was free with the place with friends who wanted to use it for a week at a time.

It was desolate up there. About two miles past town a single-lane road sliced through a stand of trees. The road was rough and pitted and it curled into a kind of S before it reached open rocky land. The road ran for about eight-tenths of a mile. Past the trees, the rocky land opened up like a fan. Higher, up a steep incline, a walk that winded almost everyone who climbed it, was the cabin. It was built with the back flush against a sheer drop of about a thousand feet.

It was first light when we forced our way up the path to the front door of the cabin. The hard climb made worse by the fact that we carried enough weapons to start a small banana-republic war. The key was where my friend had said it was, under the doormat. I tripped the heavy padlock and we went in. There was a dusty smell in the closed-off rooms. No electricity. No refrigeration. In the central room, the combination kitchen, dining room, and living room, there was a fireplace about six feet wide and four feet high. A fire was laid on the irons and there was a full wood box off to the side.

I lit a kerosene lamp and took a fast look around. Runt crouched in front of the fireplace and set the kindling going with his cigarette lighter.

"It's like a boy scout camp-out," Edward said.

"Only they bring food with them," Hump said.

"We'll drive down and stock up in an hour or so," I said. I took the lamp and went into the other room. It was the bedroom, furnished with a brass double bed and a single cot. Beyond that was a bathroom. The one convenience was the septic tank. I guess they hadn't wanted to endure an outhouse.

I found some sheets and blankets packed away in heavy plastic. I threw a couple of sheets and blankets on each bed and I was making the beds when Runt came in and stood watching, a cigarette drooping out of the corner of his mouth.

"What do you think of it?"

"Might do," he said. "I'll pace it out after a while, but I think that's a hell of a killing ground out there, where the road ends: the rock ground and the approach to the house." He moved to the cot and lifted one of the sheets and sniffed at it. "How long do you think we've got?"

"A day. A day and a half. After that, they'll know where we are."

"You sure of that?"

I nodded. "It gets leaked late tonight."

"How?"

"One of Art Maloney's pigeons."

"He the cop?"

"Yeah."

"Nice touch," he said.

"Of course."

At nine I drove alone back into Harper Falls. I'd have taken Edward with me but he was worn out after the trip. I left him sleeping in the brass double bed. I told Hump, until I was sure we could trust Runt, I wanted one of us, him or me, near Edward at all times. When I left the cabin, Hump had the loaded shotgun on the kitchen table. He was starting a fire in the old wood cookstove.

At the Apex Supermarket, really a large general store, I bought enough canned food to last at least four days: canned meats and fruit, bread and butter, eggs and bacon, and a number of tall cans of juice. At the last minute, I added a case of soft drinks and four cases of beer.

While the owner and his helper loaded down the trunk and the back seat, I took a walk around town. I spent some time looking into the display window of a mountain craft shop. There, spread out, was a beautiful homemade quilt. It was applique with a large floral design in the center and bluebirds at the corners. Whatever mountain woman had put the quilt together had matched the design on a pair of pillow cases.

I made a note to buy one for Marcy before we headed back for Atlanta. She hadn't been too happy when I'd called and told her about the trip. The quilt might cost better than a hundred but it would be worth it if it got me past Marcy's anger. Of course she put up with a lot from me.

It would have been an optimistic gesture to buy it right then and carry it back up to the cabin. It would have said something about how sure I was of the outcome. But deep in me, the part that doesn't lie, I knew the odds were about fifty-fifty against me coming back down the mountain. The quilt was too beautiful to end up with blood on it.

Hump made the first breakfast, bacon and scrambled eggs and toast browned in the oven, and coffee made in the huge old enamel coffee pot. Runt came in while Hump was dishing it out. He was wearing a .45 army automatic in an old flapped leather holster. He carried a large piece of paper wadded in one hand.

"Finished the scout," he said.

Over coffee, after we'd eaten, Runt smoothed out the sheet of paper. He'd drawn a map of the area and he'd paced off the distances. While Hump and I leaned over the table, he ran his finger over the drawing. "The only way up here is the road. Unless they're mountain climbers. Unless they've got a copter. I doubt both of those, so it's the road. Starting tonight, I'll be down on the road or one of you will, spelling me. We've got to hope they'll come up the road, at least part of the way, by car. That way we'll hear them. It'll give us time to box them." He touched squares he'd drawn on both sides of the road, about a hundred yards before the road terminated with the rocky fan that led to the cabin. "I'd like to have fire pits here and here. The problem is that it's almost solid rock. Maybe something can be done with the natural cover. But most natural cover won't stop a round."

"Sandbags?" I said.

"If we had the bags." His finger outlined the fan-shaped clearing that fronted the cabin. "This is the killing ground. Whoever's out in the fire pits when they come drives them this way, not back down the road toward town. Drives them into fire from the high ground, the cabin door and the window. There's no cover and no place to hide."

I backed away and dropped my empty coffee cup into the dishpan of water heating on the stove. "I'd like to walk through it with you."

"Now's good as any time." He stood up and moved toward the bedroom where Edward was still sleeping. I followed him and stood in the doorway. He passed the bed where Edward was and squatted in front of his foot locker. He swung the top open and pulled out a flat canvas pack. He swung the pack over one shoulder as he came back to me. "Is he worth all this?" he asked, nodding toward Edward.

"He doesn't think so. I do."

He edged past me into the kitchen. I went over and shook Edward by the shoulder. "Breakfast."

He grunted and sat up. "Pour the coffee," he mumbled.

Runt was already outside when I passed through the kitchen. Hump put a plate and cup on the table and said, "Runt seems to know his business."

"That's the way it looks."

"Out there, when it's dark, I'd hate to run into him. A man could end up bloodmeat."

I got the M1 carbine from the corner of the room and carried it out with me. Runt waited for me at the mouth of the road. He looked at the carbine and shook his head.

"Think of me as an officer."

We walked down the road about a thousand yards. Runt stopped and toed a line in the rock and dirt. "I think this is about as far as they'd come in a car. Maybe not this far. But if they're city, they might not like walking." He turned and we walked back toward the cabin. About a hundred yards before the road ended in the clearing, he stopped again. To his left as he faced the cabin, a dead tree leaned across, touching another one. "This is where I'd set up a fire pit of some kind." He stepped off the road and eased the pack to the ground next to the dead tree. He was bent over and now he froze and whipped his head toward me. "Hear something?"

He didn't wait for me to answer. He uncoiled. A leap and he was over the dead tree and crouching. The flap was open and the .45 eased out. I didn't hear anything but I followed him. Mine wasn't a graceful move. It was more a lunge than a leap. I skinned an elbow and a knee. I duckwalked toward him. "What is it?"

"Car coming," he said.

I untaped one of the clips, pointed the carbine skyward, and rammed the clip home. I charged the carbine, putting a round in the chamber.

"They're early," Runt said.

No answer for that. They were.

A minute later a black Mustang pulled level with us. Runt lifted the .45 but I put a hand on his wrist. "Not him."

I'd had my look at the driver. It was Art Maloney. By the time Runt and I reached him, he'd taken a suitcase and a riot gun out of the car. He slammed the trunk down and waited for us.

"You get lonesome, Art?"

"I took a couple of days off. You got some spare breakfast?"

"The chow's the best thing here."

I introduced Art and Runt and they nodded at each other. Art turned and walked up the hill toward the cabin. Runt and I brought up the rear.

"Hardman, I hope you like jungle warfare."

"Huh?"

"The odds just swung toward us. With him here, Maloney, you're down in the barrel with me. Full time."

"Hump might be better," I said. I knew it wasn't true, but I wanted to see what Runt would say.

"Not in this army. Butt-stomping and ass-kicking, he'd be first team. But not back there."

"Why?"

He stopped and faced back toward the road. "Up here, from the cabin, if they get this far, you kill to keep from being killed, self-defense, and almost anybody kills when they have to." He pointed a finger down the road. "In the fire pits it'll be cold blood. You won't like it, Hardman, but you'll do it."

"What makes you so sure?"

He grinned, showing small yellow teeth. "I heard. The paper said security men killed three men trying to rob that Tower. That was the cover. I heard different. You cut one with a piece and shredded two others with a shotgun."

"They'd killed a sick old man," I said. I don't know why I was arguing. From him it was a compliment of sorts.

"The two you got with the shotgun ... facing you or heading away?"

"Facing me, but blinded by a light."

"You see?"

I did.

"Explain it to me, Art."

It was late afternoon. Runt was down the road about a hundred yards near the fallen tree. He'd been working since lunch on the fire pit, using large stones to construct a wall. Now he'd finished and he was covering the wall with rotten wood and underbrush so it couldn't be seen from the road.

"Something bothered me."

Back in the cabin, I could hear Hump and Edward playing poker with a greasy deck Hump had found in the kitchen.

"What?"

"Ed Penny. You were talking with him at the Gray Horse Tavern."

"That's right."

"At two a.m. he stopped a couple in an outdoor phone booth down the road."

"Bad?"

"Not good," Art said. "When I left, he'd been operated on. He was in an intensive care ward."

"What's bothering you?"

Art nodded down the road. "Runt there."

"What about him?"

Through the cabin wall I could hear Hump whoop and holler. He'd filled a straight.

"It doesn't read right, Jim. You're getting set to face some pros and nobody wants to touch it. And in walks another pro, and he'll wade right in."

"Runt might not be a pro."

"Don't kid yourself."

"All right." I got out my pack of smokes and shook out a couple. Art cupped a match. "Maybe I got impatient. Maybe Runt's a plant. But maybe not. And I didn't get offered a lot to choose from."

"I hope Runt's straight," Art said.

"For my sake?"

"For his," Art said. "If he's not, you kill him or I do."

I let that flatten out and die between us.

Runt appeared at the end of the road, at the mouth of the rock fan opening below us. He looked up and waved. I waved and looked over at Art. He'd turned his back and gone into the cabin.

I'd lost the flip and taken the first watch, the six-to-midnight. I ate early and was making myself a sandwich to take down to the fire pit with me when Runt came in from the bedroom with a flat case a bit larger than the usual attaché case. He placed the case on a clear end of the dining table and flipped open the top. Art drifted over from the window and watched while Runt unclipped a couple of straps. He lifted out a Walther submachine gun. It was the short model, the MPK. Without the stock, it was about fifteen inches long. The stock, unfolded, added another eleven or twelve inches. That was the stock that came with the weapon. But the stock Runt took from the case and attached to the MPK was about half that length. It was a special design, with something like a bicycle grip at the back. It was made of hard rubber and had finger notches.

"You wouldn't believe the trouble I had getting this baby into the country," Runt said.

"I'd believe it," Art said.

"That's the cop talk," Runt said. He worked the bolt a couple of times and shoved a magazine home. "Had to ship it to a guy I knew in Mexico and he paid some sailors to take it over the border at T-Town."

"Automatic only?" Art said.

Runt shook his head. "It was a special order for an outfit I was with. Selective too."

"You mind?" Art held out a hand.

"Not a bit." Runt passed the MPK to him.

"You boys be careful," I said. I wrapped my sandwich and carried it and the Ml carbine down to the fire pit where Hump was waiting for me.

After dark the temperature dropped as if it had rolled over the side of a table. It was still a long way from the kind of weather it would be in December. I was warm enough with the extra shirt I'd worn under my jacket.

The time limped on. It reminded me of the watches I'd stood in Japan and Korea, boredom and the cold, without even fear and tension to keep me alert. This night's watch was just a shake-down. The word wouldn't be on the street until about midnight.

Art had arranged that before he left Atlanta. Add to that the time before the rumor reached the death squad. Add the three hours or so of driving time.

A few minutes before twelve, with legs stiff and half-asleep, I got up and stepped out of the fire pit. I did a few paces up the road and returned. I stopped a few feet from the fire pit and stretched and yawned.

Then I saw Runt. I didn't hear him. I saw him. He moved down the road toward the fire pit as if he knew every loose rock on the road and how to avoid them. He reached the fire pit and leaned toward it.

"Not there," I said.

Runt jerked around, the Walther MPK swinging toward me. At the last moment, before it was level with me, he lowered the muzzle toward the roadbed. "You playing cowboy and Indians?"

"Not me," I said.

I walked over to him.

"You be down at six, Hardman?"

"On the dot," I said.

I didn't sleep well. Hump and Art were splitting the watch at the front window. It was Art's watch from midnight to six. I had the cot while Hump and Edward shared the double bed. Both of them had a rough night of snoring. Against that, I got about two hours of sleep and two hours of rolling around. A bit after four I gave it up and dressed and went into the kitchen. Art had a pot of coffee going. It was fresh and I had a cup and waited to see if the hung-over feeling would go away.

"Quiet below?"

"So far," Art said.

"Coffee's good." I pushed back my chair and got the carbine from the corner of the room. "I'll spell Runt so he can get a cup."

"You're all heart," Art said.

"It's cold out there."

Art nodded and I went out. It was lighter now. Some of the cloud cover had blown past. It was bright enough so I could see my way down the path. With the trees on both sides, now on the road, it was a bit darker. Runt stepped out of the trees near the fire pit when I was still a few yards away.

"It six already?"

"Couldn't sleep. Art's made a fresh pot. I'll take it while you go up and have a cup."

"Thanks anyway. I'm fine without it."

"You sure?"

"Coffee gives me the shits."

I heard it this time. I was turning away when I heard the car engine heading toward us. No lights were showing and that might be why the car was coming so slowly.

"Company?"

"Huh?"

"A car."

Runt turned and ducked into the underbrush near the fire pit. I started that way and stopped. Too crowded. Instead. I made a leap for the brush across the road. Settled there, on one knee, stilling my breath, I charged the carbine and waited.

A couple of minutes passed before the car drew level with us and eased to a stop. A compact. A dark Volvo. Outside of a jeep, for this kind of road, it might have been the best choice. Right after the man cut the engine, he opened the door and stepped out. The brief flash of the inside light revealed that the man was alone. Then the door closed and it was dark again.

He stood there next to the Volvo, not moving, and I heard a noise I didn't place at first. Finally I got it. The man was pissing and the time it was taking him he must have had a full bladder.

Bent over, shielded by the car, I stepped into the road and eased my way down the length of the body, heading for the hood.

When I reached the hood, I swung the carbine around. I could see his outline. He was short and blocky. His face tipped up toward the light from the cabin. The piss thinned. Down to a thin stream.

I got ready. Ready to straighten out and turn the carbine on him. At the back of my throat was the command to freeze. Just as I tensed myself, I heard the dry and hard sound. The bolt of the Walther MPK. The man next to the Volvo heard it too. He swung around toward the fire pit. The stream of piss thundered against the side of the hood.

Runt shot him with a short burst. The force of the 9-mm rounds threw him against the hood and down into the road.

I ducked around the front of the Volvo. "Godammit, Runt, we don't even know …"

Runt stepped out of the pit. "Check the car, Hardman."

I opened the door on the driver's side and looked in. Nothing. No weapons showing.

"Runt, how do we know this is one of …?"

"He was scouting," Runt said. He pointed a flashlight down at the body. The man was face down. Runt shoved a foot under him and flipped him over. He leaned over the body and unbuttoned the hip-length car coat. When he threw the coat open, I saw the shoulder rig and the butt of the piece under the left arm. Runt straightened up. "That's their first mistake. The odds are getting better."

In the light, before he switched it off, I could see the half-moon pool of urine just beyond the man's head.

The light went out. I could hear Art calling down from the cabin doorway.

# CHAPTER TWELVE

As Runt drove the Volvo into the clearing at the foot of the cabin and backed it around, Art stood halfway up the path with his arms folded across his chest. He watched Runt drive up the road before he walked down the path and stopped next to me.

"I guess you fell off the fence, Jim."

"Looks that way." The truth was I hadn't. I was pulled in both directions. Runt had killed the man and that ought to make me believe in him. Still, it hadn't been necessary. I'd had him cold.

"Just because he did the killing?"

"For him it's that way. Kill first and then take the census."

"Think about it," Art said. "The man he killed could have been a drinking friend of his, if they're part of the same death squad."

"Why would he do that?"

"You walked into it. You messed it up. That dude was crossed out anyway, no use anymore."

"Why him? Why not take me out?"

"It wouldn't get him a home-free shot at Edward." He hawked and spat on the ground in front of us.

"And if this doesn't?"

"Sooner or later, he'll make his try anyway," Art said.

"Tell me this, Art. You rather have him here where you can watch him, or out there, walking quiet, coming at you from any direction or any time?"

"Your way, Jim."

It wasn't my way at all. Not really. But it was a fairly good recovery.

From the cabin doorway, Hump called Art up to breakfast.

The MPK was propped up against the side of the fire pit wall. Next to that were the web belt and the empty flap holster where Runt had tossed it when he'd stuffed the .45 army issue in his jacket pocket. It seemed right but something was missing. It took me a few minutes of running it back through my head before I remembered. The flat pack that Runt had slung over his shoulder the day before, after he'd made his scout, when we'd walked over the ground. I'd hadn't seen it since.

It took me ten minutes to find it. I walked a series of half-circles, away from the fire pit, away from the road, each time broadening the hunt until I found it in a pocket dug out under a rotting tree. Leaves and trash covered the opening.

I pulled it out and stood up. Inside there were about ten hard chocolate bars held together by a rubber band, two spare clips for the .45, four grenades, and a walkie-talkie. It was an expensive model, the type a police department might use, not a child's toy, not Radio Shack.

I put it all back into the pack and strapped it up again. After I shoved it back into the hole, I covered it once more with leaves and trash.

Back at the side of the road, I kept trying it out. I ran it through the needle's eye a number of times. I didn't like any way it came out

It was forty minutes or so before I heard Runt trotting up the road. When he saw me step into the road he slowed to a walk. Reaching me, he'd slowed his breathing down until it was almost regular. "I found an old house off a side road. Nobody there.

Looks like it's been empty for a month or so. I left the Volvo there, back in a stand of trees."

"No sign?"

He shook his head. "Road looks clean all the way back into town."

"You go that far?"

"Half the way. I didn't find a place to dump the car, so I turned and came back."

"And found the side road?"

He nodded. He stepped off the road and leaned over and lifted the Walther submachine gun out of the fire pit. "I need four hours sleep. The watch is yours until then."

"Four on and four off?"

"Until dark," he said. "After that nobody sleeps."

"Tonight?"

"If I was running it," he said.

I watched him walk up the path to the cabin: young, not showing the effects of the night watch and the two or three miles of trot. I'd been that way once. It had been a long time ago.

Maybe you are running it, Runt. Just maybe.

Just in case he was, I didn't use the fire pit. I took a position across the road from it and sat with my back to a tree. The sun warmed me and it wasn't a bad watch. A bit before ten, I stood up and stretched and walked over to the fire pit. I was waiting there for Runt when he came down from the cabin.

I didn't sleep. Hump had the watch at the window. Art was in the bedroom stretched out on the cot, eyes open, staring up at the ceiling. Edward owned the kitchen. After he washed the breakfast dishes, he cleared off the table and got out the deck of cards. I sat across from him and kept him company with a few hands of five card stud.

"Who was the dead man?"

I said I didn't know.

"I guess I didn't know until now."

I asked what he was talking about.

"Why we came up here."

I knew he'd figure it out sooner or later.

"I'm fifty-one now."

I said I'd guessed his age somewhere around there, give or take a year or two.

"That's old enough to know what I want."

I nodded.

"You lied to me, Hardman."

I shrugged.

"You said there wouldn't be any more killing."

Hump turned from the window. "It's out of his hands. That old man cut his dogs loose before he died."

"I could walk out of here," Edward said.

"If you can get past me," Hump said.

"I'm sick of this."

"I'm not laughing either," I said.

Edward dropped the deck of cards on the table and walked into the bedroom. A few seconds later I heard the shoes dropping and the creak of the bedsprings.

"He's getting his rest," Hump said.

"Aren't we all?"

"Art's not. You missed it."

"Missed what?" I walked over to the window and stood next to him, staring out at the sky. A light rain was falling.

"Art and Runt almost got it on a while ago."

"Before he came down?"

"About then," Hump said.

"What about?"

"Art had a wild hair going. Runt sat there at the table cleaning that submachine gun of his. When he had it back together he stood up and walked behind Art, about the same time he was putting the magazine back in. Art didn't like it. He told Runt to stay in front of him. He wanted it from the front."

"And Runt?"

"Runt laughed at him and told Art the chicken was pecking at his guts."

"That's as far as it got?"

Hump nodded. "I stomped on it."

"Risky," I said.

"Not really," Hump said. "For some reason, neither one of them was quite ready to let it slip all the way."

Sure. Art holding back because he knew I'd rather have Runt around where I could watch him, Runt because he wasn't about to risk it all with Art, not when the real job hadn't been done.

I let it drop with Hump. I got out a big pot and opened a couple of big cans of beef stew. I poured in a small bottle of A-1 and broke up a dried red pepper from a string on the wall next to the fireplace. I placed that on the back of the stove to simmer. That was lunch.

Art stumbled in about one-thirty, red-eyed, still without any sleep. I dipped him out a bowl of the stew and placed it in front of him with a cup of coffee and the platter of light bread.

After one bite Art said, "Jesus, this is awful."

"Suffer it," I said. "Runt thinks it'll be over tonight."

"That little crap head."

"I hear you've been pushing him."

"Some. I wanted to see what he'd do."

"And?"

"He's playing for the right time."

"You sure?"

"Sure as I know my name."

I leaned across the table and dropped my voice so Hump couldn't hear us. "One more item for that love letter you're writing him. He's got a walkie-talkie hidden away out there."

"That's it." Art took one more bite from the bowl of stew and pushed it away. "You know that's it."

"Some things bother me."

"I'll tick them off for you. Here's this dude's supposed to be a pro, comes tooling down the road like he knows where he's going. Knows exactly. So relaxed he gets out of the car and starts taking a three-minute piss. Not a worry in the world, just waiting for Runt to step out and show himself. The only thing is that you've picked that time to be a nice guy and go down and offer to spell Runt while he has a cup of coffee." He looked up at me. "He try to run you off?"

I nodded. "Said coffee gives him the runs."

"Hump?" Art looked past me.

I turned and found Hump right behind me. "He drinks it by the gallon at all meals," Hump said.

"So Runt's got a problem. You. Hell, it wouldn't bother him if you got the drop on that guy and captured him. It would put one more man up in the cabin. What bothered him was that that dude was going to holler his name out loud."

It had the right sound to it. I'd been thinking some of the same things while I waited for him to come back from dumping the car and the body. "No walkie-talkie in the car that I could see."

"That means the rest of the squad is parked a couple of miles away, within range. Runt calls in and tells them he thinks five a.m. might be a good time for a move. He might have planned to take you out when you relieved him at six."

"How do you see it?"

"That one comes up first. He and Runt off you. He leaves the fire pit and comes up to the house. He says he's tired and he's going to sack out. He tells one of us, me or Hump, to go down and spell you for breakfast in an hour or so. By then the rest of the squad is in place. Either Hump or I walk into the buzz-saw. Then it's Runt up here. Against either me or Hump. Short odds.

A couple of bursts later from that submachine gun and they're home free."

"Sounds likely," Hump said.

I looked at my watch. Quarter to two. About time for me to take the watch in the fire pit.

"I think it's time we have a talk with Runt."

I nodded. It was past time if Art had it figured right.

I stopped about twenty yards from the fire pit. It was still raining and ruts were getting a bit deep in rain water. "Runt?"

He didn't answer. Behind me and to my right Art lifted the police-issue riot gun and pumped a shell into it.

"Runt?"

Still no answer. Art moved up on my hip. "I think he's been spooked."

Art took a couple of steps forward. I caught him just in time and grabbed him by the arm and jerked him back.

"What the hell, Jim?"

"There." I pointed down at the place where the rain had washed away the dirt on the top ridge of one of the ruts. A thin black wire showed against the red clay mud. "I forgot to tell you there were four grenades in the pack with the walkie-talkie."

"You feel like disarming them?"

"Out of my league," I said.

Art touched my arm and waved me back toward the cabin. He followed me and when we were about fifty yards from the point where I'd seen the black wire, Art put the shotgun to his shoulder and took a kneeling position. The first round broke the wire. Grenades went off on both sides of the road.

As soon as the echo died down, I walked past Art and looked at the damage. Underbrush had been ripped away on both sides of the road, for about ten yards each way.

Art was right. Runt had spooked. The fire pit was empty and the pack was gone from its hiding place. There wasn't any way of knowing how long he'd been gone.

# CHAPTER THIRTEEN

In the late afternoon, I rode with Art as far as the end of the private road. I pushed the door open when he stopped the Mustang but I didn't get out right away. With one arm on the seat back, I could see the top of Edward's head. He was down in the floorboards.

"Keep down," I said. "All the way to the police station."

"He will." Art clawed my shirt pocket and got out my pack. "He will, if he wants his head in one piece."

Before we left the cabin, Hump and Edward had smoked a joint or two. Now he was loose and easy. "You're fired, Hardman. All of you."

"I wasn't even hired," Art said.

Edward laughed. "I think I'm getting crazy as the rest of you."

"Hold that thought." I got back my pack of smokes and tossed Art a twenty. "A reason for the trip. Bring back three steaks and the makings."

"Big ones?"

"We might as well do the hardy meal thing."

I backed into the tree cover and watched Art's Mustang follow the highway toward Harper Falls. I gave it ten minutes. At the end of that time, when no car passed heading for town, I walked back up the road to the cabin.

Our thinking ran this way: Runt was my mistake and we had to live with it. Still, he knew too much. All the scouting he'd done around the approach to the cabin, the measuring and the pacing, the figuring of the angles of fire, had been for the death squad. It was for the backup plan in case the first attempt failed. And it had. I'd stumbled into the middle and spoiled it. It had cost the squad a man, the man Runt had to kill to protect himself.

In ordinary circumstances, Runt would have remained with us, taking his time, waiting for an opening. Since he didn't, I believed that he'd seen that the odds had gone the wrong way. The arrival of Art had meant he couldn't do the job alone. He couldn't off Edward and hope to get away untouched. Before, when there had been just Hump and me, it was possible. He could take me out down at the fire pit, using some quiet method, and then walk up to the cabin. He'd catch Hump off guard and off him. After that Edward would be easy. But with Art and Hump at the cabin at all times, the inside way wouldn't go.

Added to that, Art hadn't bought Runt's cover. He'd shown how suspicious he was. So Runt had talked to the others on the walkie-talkie and they'd pulled him out. To regroup, I guess. The grenade ambush had been Runt's good-bye and thank-you note.

It had been Art's idea to squirrel Edward away for the night. He'd drive Edward to the Harper Falls police station, show his I.D., and do a tap dance about Edward being a witness against a big rackets man in Atlanta. For his safety, Art wanted him kept overnight in the station. He'd flash around some money I'd given him and offer to pay fifty dollars a man for any special policemen the chief would put on to guard Edward that night.

With Edward out of the way, we could settle in for the bloodbath on the mountain. Handled right, they'd believe Edward was still at the cabin and they'd have to come after him. They couldn't wait forever.

Art returned from town about an hour later. He'd done his shopping. The three huge T-bone steaks had probably been cut from some local gully-jumper cow or other. The baking potatoes weighed about a pound each and there was a ball of homemade butter with the mold stamp on it.

Art stayed down on the road with me while Hump stoked up the wood stove and put the potatoes in the oven. It would be an hour or so before we could eat. Knowing the quality of the usual gully-jumper beef, I wasn't sure it would be worth the effort.

As he'd expected, the local chief had been pleased to be helpful to the big city cop. The first calls the chief made located two deer hunters who'd said they'd load their deer rifles and be right over. Fifty dollars was good pay for something most of these mountain men did for the fun of it. That is, sitting around and smoking, chewing and telling lies, with a bottle of some kind of pop-skull to rinse their mouths out with now and then.

He'd taken his care going to the police station. He was sure no one followed him. But twenty or thirty minutes later he'd picked up a tail at the grocery store. A black Buick was across the street when he came out and it had followed him back to the private road.

"Get a look at them?"

"Not a close one," Art said, "but close enough to see that neither of the two was Runt."

"That's three then. At least three."

"Like the F.B.I. thought. A four-man squad, minus the one Runt burned."

I grinned at him. "Nice of Runt."

"Oh, he was a sweetheart."

After the rain, it was cooler now. A strong wind fingered and searched us. Up at the cabin sparks blew from the roof chimney.

We ate in shifts: Hump was first, and when he was done, he put Art's steak in the huge old skillet and came down to keep me company while Art cooked it to his taste and ate it. Art passed me on the path and said the steak was tough as plywood.

I took my time. I pounded my steak with the edge of a saucer and then I put about half of the butter left into the skillet. I added some fat kindling to the stove and when the stove lid was cherry red, I put the lid aside and cooked the steak right over the flames. I gave it a burned crust on both sides and tipped the steak out on a plate. After all that trouble, it was still about as tough as wet plywood.

I'd pushed the bone aside and was eating the potato crust when I heard the first gunfire. Art pumped the riot gun as fast as he could. A rip from an automatic weapon. That was followed by both barrels of Hump's tree-killer.

I scooped the kerosene lamp from the corner of the table and ducked away from the window. I trimmed the wick until there was only a feeble light left. Still bent over, I placed the lamp on the floor below the window. The Ml carbine was next to the door. I grabbed it and held it against my hip to charge it. Ready. A deep breath and I swung the door open a foot or so and stepped out sideways, bent over, pulling the door closed behind me. Not slamming it, easing it shut.

I crouched with my back to the cabin wall. The feeble light from the window didn't touch me. I waited, with eyes closed for a few seconds and then opened. I wouldn't rush it. I knew my night sight would be better soon. Down below me, in the road, was a flash and the flattened-out echo rattled off the cabin wall.

With my eyes better now, I could see the fringe of the wood below, the thick stand of trees sliced apart by the road, starlight pale on the rock fan of the killing ground. Ready as I'd ever be, I stood up and felt my thighs shaking, the strain of holding the crouch too long. I rubbed one leg and then the other. Patient, waiting, I noticed the silence below. It was like a truce. I counted it out. When I reached sixty, an automatic weapon ripped out a long burst. Hump's tree-killer roared back.

Time. I felt for the path and started down. The rocks were slick from the afternoon rain. I was still counting, not aware that I was, until I reached sixty and the automatic weapons tore the silence. I stopped. It was a pattern I didn't understand and it bothered me. An odd kind of war: the shotguns and the automatic weapons, both effective at rock-throwing distance, were standing off and shooting the hell out of the trees in no man's land.

Counting again, I reached sixty and the automatic weapons underscored it. Once it could be an accident. Three times it was a definite pattern. I turned and went back up the path. I stood with my back to the door. After two more repetitions of the pattern I ducked under the window casing and took my position at the corner of the cabin.

This time when I reached sixty, the first mistake in the pattern. Silence, no gunfire, and I heard, below me and to the right, the sound of one rock grinding against another one. At sixty-three an automatic weapon cut in. Too late. I'd heard it. Someone had worked their way through the woods, circling Art and Hump's position. It could be a movement to flank Art and Hump, but I didn't think so. No, whoever was down there was after the cabin, after Edward. The defensive fire below revealed that two of us were down by the road. That meant they'd only have to get past the third defender to reach Edward. It was the best setup they could expect. Get past the gun at the cabin, kill Edward, and they could vanish in the woods, to appear in a few days in New York or Chicago or God knows where.

Cold wind, but I could feel the sweat break, into thin runs down my sides, ice on my forehead. Hardly breathing, I waited for the second mistake. I didn't count any more. It wasn't necessary. I'd tagged it and I knew they'd set up a one-minute pattern. The man coming toward me now counted along with them and moved on the mark of sixty, using the sound to cover any noise of his passage.

Goose and gander. I used the gunfire as he did. I moved out, away from the corner of the cabin. I wanted a better angle of fire toward the cabin door. Satisfied, I bellied down on the rock, the carbine at my shoulder, elbows dug into the rock. I sighted in on the door. The angle up was slight, about where I thought Runt's chest would be.

Two more minutes, two more bursts. I was surprised when it came. I still hadn't placed him on the path. A kick and the cabin door flew open. I caught the outline of the man in the faint light. A bigger man than Runt stood there. He was dressed all in black, over six feet tall and he was older, near fifty. As soon as the door swung open he pulled trigger on an MPK and turned the weapon, stitching his way across the front room.

I knew I didn't have much time. I had a second or a split of one. I didn't bother to adjust the angle I'd set ahead of time. If I waited, he'd move out of the doorway. I squeezed trigger and emptied about half of the magazine, seven or eight rounds. I hit him about thigh high. The force of the rounds that hit him broke him low and threw him against the doorframe. But he wasn't done. He bounced away and swung the MPK toward me. He was falling and his finger stayed on the trigger. He sprayed the rocks below, the barrel edging toward me. My luck. He was dying, probably, and it looked like he might take me under with him. I pulled the carbine toward me and rolled for the corner of the cabin. As I bumped into the cabin, the ear-breaking sound ended. I heard him grunting, holding back the scream of pain. So that was it. The magazine held thirty rounds or so, give or take a couple, and he'd used them up. Too much firepower into the empty cabin. I pushed the carbine toward him and emptied the rest of the magazine into the lump form in the doorway.

No sound after that. No grunting. I broke the tape and got the spare magazine free from the stock. I pulled out the empty and jammed the replacement home. I charged it before I got to my knees and crawled toward the doorway. Reaching him, I put the carbine aside and used both hands to drag the body out of the light. No noises from him. I found his throat and felt for a pulse. None.

There was still a dim light from the open doorway. Just outside the door I could see the MPK. It wasn't like Runt's. It had the standard eleven- or twelve-inch folding metal rod stock. Might as well. I sucked it up and stepped over the body. With one hand I grabbed the MPK. With the other I caught the door latch and jerked it shut.

It was an unfamiliar weapon, one I'd never fired. I fumbled with it until I got the empty magazine free. That done, I patted the body down until I found a spare in a pouch at the man's belt.

I rammed the spare home and worked the bolt until I had a round in the chamber. Below me, down near the road, another exchange of fire. Runt was down there. Damn him. And I got the ghost of an idea. The last they'd heard from the cabin had been my carbine. It would mean I'd come out with the edge. I wanted to change that impression. I braced the stock of the MPK against my shoulder and fired a short burst of eight or ten rounds.

With the carbine in one hand and the MPK in the other, I ran down the path toward the trees, hoping I wouldn't run into Art or Hump. They'd heard that final burst and they'd make their guess what the silence after that meant.

Dark in the trees. Getting wet, I moved through the underbrush. Deep in the woods, I used the exchange of fire again, this time to cover my approach, using a wide circle at first to keep me out of the range of the shotguns Art and Hump were firing, just in case they heard me. After a hundred yards or so I swung left, pointing toward the flash of the weapons. Five minutes. Then ten minutes.

Careful. Still, he was there before I expected him. I stepped past a stand of trees and I saw the muzzle flash. I was behind him and to his right if he turned. I eased down to one knee and placed the carbine on the ground, flat against my down leg. I lifted the MPK. As I leaned forward a dry-rotted limb broke under my weight.

"Mace? That you?"

It wasn't Runt's voice. I grunted what might have passed for a yes.

"Get him?"

I grunted again.

I could hear the fear. "Is that you, Mace? Say something."

I couldn't see him. All I had to go on was the memory of the position where I'd seen the muzzle flash. I pointed the MPK a few feet forward of that and burned the rest of the magazine swinging it back toward him. I didn't hit him. I guess he'd dropped as soon as he had decided my grunts weren't the best identification. He waited until he was sure the magazine was empty and then he panicked. Confused or just too afraid to care, he jumped to his feet and ran toward the road. I dropped the MPK and brought up the carbine. I didn't fire. I didn't want to put any rounds in the general direction of Art and Hump. And I didn't have to. Art's riot gun and Hump's shotgun fired at about the same time.

Two down. The wild panic running ended. That left Runt.

I waited.

A minute. Another minute. I didn't have to count. The tick was in me. I'd had practice. Not that it really mattered. Runt would have to break soon. He was outgunned and he knew it.

First, I wasn't sure. A soft dragging sound. It was straight ahead, some yards beyond the point where I'd fired the MPK at the second man. I waited. That sound again. I knew it now: soft walking on wet, soggy leaves. This second time, unless the darkness fooled me, he was moving away from me, in the direction of the highway, about a half-mile to go.

The sound again. I lifted the carbine and squeezed off a round. It set him off. He wasn't walking any more. It was a headlong rush. I squeezed off a couple of rounds. I heard him fall and the desperate scrabbling in the undergrowth. Only seconds later, he was up and running again. I didn't follow. I leaned against a tree and listened to the noise of the running get fainter and fainter in the distance. It ended and I stepped away from the tree.

"Hump? Art? It's clear over here."

On the way to the road, passing the fire pit, I saw the chewed-up body of the man who'd panicked. I didn't take a long look. I'd seen enough bodies in the last couple of weeks.

Art almost knocked me over with his rush to me. He wrapped an arm around me. "You scared hell out of us."

"Couldn't call you on the phone," I said.

Hump tapped me on the shoulder on the way to the body. He took a long look at the man, maybe the first man he'd had a part in killing, and bent over, gagging. It hadn't been good steak anyway.

Sheriff Abel Box didn't like us one bit. A banty little man with a beer gut and a pigeon chest, he'd arrived within minutes of the last round I'd fired. Watching him, listening to him, I had the feeling he'd have shot the three of us himself if he could think of some way of explaining it.

After we walked it through for him, Hump and Art took him up to the cabin for a cup of coffee. I didn't go with them. I rode out to the highway with Box's deputy. We parked and got out and walked. After a few minutes of walking, we found the tire treads deep in mud, where they'd parked their car. And the deputy, pointing his flashlight toward the woods, showed me where Runt had skidded in the mud and gone down. I guess the deputy was another of those deer hunters. While I stood and watched, he went into the woods for a few feet and came back with a couple of leaves in the palm of his hand. When he pointed the light at his hand, I could see that there were smears of blood on the leaves. So I'd nicked him. Or someone had.

Back at the cabin the coffee was ready. I poured myself a cup and walked around, looking at the damage the burst from the MPK had done. It had ripped up part of the wall and chipped away at the fireplace. All this time Art droned away at Sheriff Box. In the end the sheriff bought it. It was either that or arrest all of us. That meant trials and expense to the county. Rather than that, he wrote it off as a professional hit try that had gone bad.

We followed Sheriff Box down into Harper Falls. While Hump and Art collected Edward from the police station and paid off the deer hunters, I registered for four rooms at the best motel in town. Even before they arrived, I'd had a shower and stretched out in bed. I went over the edge as if I weighed at least a ton.

After breakfast Edward left for Atlanta with Art. Hump and I stayed behind long enough to clean up the cabin as well as we could. On the way back through town, I asked around and found a carpenter who said he'd repair the damage to the cabin. I told him what was involved and he set a price. I upped his price about twenty percent, just in case, and told him where to leave the key when the work was done.

My last stop in town was at the craft shop. I paid a hundred and twenty-five dollars for the quilt in the window, the one with the floral design in the center and the bluebirds. The matching pillow cases came with it.

The war was over. We took our time driving back to Atlanta.

# CHAPTER FOURTEEN

The call came three nights later. It was a few minutes after midnight. It was raining in Atlanta, a cold brittle rain like ice. It was a sound that had rocked both Marcy and me to sleep. And then the phone rang.

"You're hard to find, Hardman."

"You've been looking for me?" I recognized the voice, the faint twang in it. Or I'd been expecting him to get in touch with me.

"Not really."

"Tell me about it, Runt."

"You put a hole in me, Hardman."

"It wasn't any more than you'd have done for me," I said.

He started to laugh but I guess that gave him some pain. He choked it off. "I guess you know I came into some money. I've retired."

The hundred thousand dollar payment from Alec Troutman. As the last one alive it all fell to him. "You sure?"

"I bought myself a bar."

"Where?"

"You've got to be kidding, Hardman."

"Just testing," I said.

"The reason I called is," he said, "now that I'm out of it I wanted to find out how good your memory is."

"It's rotten."

"Give me an example," Runt said.

"Let's see." I felt Marcy stirring behind me. "You're six-one or two. Dark hair. Two hundred and ten or so. And you look like a redneck copy of Paul Newman."

"Anything else you remember?"

"There's a bullet hole in your hide somewhere but I don't remember where I was aiming at the time."

"And Hump and Art?"

"The same," I said. "Maybe even worse."

"Go back to sleep." Runt hung up on me.

Resting on one elbow, with the slow kind smile of a woman sure of herself and of me on her face, Marcy said, "Who was that, at this time of the night?"

"A girl who wants to get in my pants."

"Why would she want to do that?"

We hugged and outlaughed the steady rain.

It was an item that didn't make the Atlanta newspapers. It came in a plain envelope that had a New York City postmark, a clipping and nothing else.

DALLAS, TEXAS (UPI) Franklin L. Clark, an executive with the Troutman Oil of Texas Company, was killed early this morning in his downtown Dallas apartment. He had been shot twice at close range with a handgun. From the way the apartment had been searched and the fact that a number of art objects were missing, Dallas police theorized that Clark surprised a thief in his apartment...

I tore up the clipping and flushed it down the john.

So Runt had retired, at least for the time. His last act had been to punch Clark's ticket. With Troutman dead and Clark gone too, there wasn't anyone to ask for a refund or insist that Runt form another team and carry out the contract. Neat. It was a kind of professional neatness.

The next day I called the Templeton apartments at the Melton Towers. All I could find out was that Beth Fanzia was in Europe and Edward was in Arizona. They wouldn't give out either address.

THE END

# AFTERWORD

## "Ralph"
## By Cynthia Williams

I knew Ralph Dennis first as a teacher, and later as a friend and mentor. Eventually, he asked me to marry him, but I refused, and our friendship ended.

Obviously, I will remember Ralph differently from the men who knew him, because he was, in some ways, a different person with me.

I met Ralph Dennis in 1966. I was in my junior year at UNC-Chapel Hill, majoring in Radio, Television and Motion Picture Production (RTVMP), and as my rather vague intent was to become a screenwriter for motion pictures, I took Mr. Dennis's screenplay writing classes. He was a good teacher, because I still remember the mechanics of writing a film script, yet all I remember of the classes is Ralph sitting on the edge of his desk, coffee cup in one hand and a cigarette in the other, his face expressionless, occasionally flicking cigarette ash at an ashtray. In retrospect, I suspect he may have been bored. Possibly hung over.

I liked him. He was cool. I saw him as a Hemingway-esque kind of writer. Undoubtedly, he did, too.

After I graduated in 1968, some circumstance I don't recall brought me back to Chapel Hill while Ralph was still teaching. I remember only that we met in his hangout, a small bar on the downslope of west Franklin Street. Ralph sat across the booth from me and my young husband, clearly uncomfortable.

I intuited that I should not have brought Dewey with me. I came away from the meeting with an inexplicable sense of dissatisfaction, the feeling that I had embarrassed the man—or worse, bored him.

Four or five years later, in 1974, I was divorced, living in east-central Tennessee, and working on my first novel. By this time, Ralph had left UNC and was living some 200 miles away from me in Atlanta, trying to make it as a self-supporting writer. I have no idea how I knew where he was, unless we had kept up some kind of occasional correspondence. So many links are missing from my recollections of this time that I can scarcely connect the dots between one event and the next. Not that it matters. All I know is that over the next two years, I drove down to Atlanta a few times to spend a weekend carousing with Ralph and friends of his (including that insanely funny Ben Jones) at George's Deli.

I recall his apartment as being one large room above a garage. As you walked in, his writing desk was to your right. To your left was a small bathroom. Beyond that, to the left, a book case and against the far wall a single-size bed. There must have been some kind of cooking facility and a table because on the one occasion I visited him there, he made shrimp scampi for me—shrimp sautéed in butter with scallions—served with a cold white wine.

I must have brought my unfinished manuscript with me that day, because I remember sitting on the edge of his bed while he sat at his desk reading it. I dared not even look at him while he read.

Finally, he stirred. I put my face in my hands as he got up with the manuscript in his hand and walked across the room to me. He stood over me with his gentle smile. "Lady," he said, "this is a hardback."

We walked in the park across the street one brisk, bright, golden autumn day. Ralph was rather stiffly polite, so I think it was probably during my first visit to him there. In my company, he was always a gentleman. Kind. Gentle. Smiling. Perhaps in deference to my youth and obvious naiveté. I was intelligent and well-educated, but when it came to knowing men, I was dumb as a post.

I was beautiful, you see, with a voluptuous body of which I was oblivious. I was entirely cerebral, impassioned with the life of the intellect. In my eyes, Ralph was still my teacher. He was sending me the books he said were required reading if I seriously wanted to learn how to write. The first book he sent me was Dostoyevsky's *The Idiot.* Told me to read it every year, as he did. He introduced me to Turgenev with *A Sportsman's Sketches.* All of the titles on his reading list were classics, heavy, rich literature. I wallowed in them with such pleasure, with an insatiable appetite for learning. And I was excited by his interest in me as a writer.

The seduction he practiced upon me was patient. Patiently, over a cheesy French onion soup with a bottle of strong, raw Chianti, he listened, smiling, to my passionate opinions about God-knows-what-all. When he spoke, always quietly and deliberately, I was an eager listener. He must have been encouraged by the warm light in my eyes, unsuspecting that it was the glow of admiration, perhaps affection, but not desire.

Every morning while our friendship lasted, he wrote a letter to me. Called it his ten-finger exercise—a warm-up for the day's writing. I have none of the letters he wrote to me, and of them, I recall only one; he described a recent date involving "one of those sweaty, candlelight suppers" that Southern women insisted upon.

Ralph was a disciplined writer and he had to be, because his income from the Hardman books depended on the quantity of his output. He was clearly embarrassed to be writing for money, restless and angry at the necessity of it, hoping to make enough from the Hardman books to support himself while he wrote some serious hardbacks. He described his life as being a routine of writing by day and drinking beer at George's by night.

Ralph sent me copies of all the Hardman books with affectionate inscriptions, but like the Valentine's Day gift of *The*

*Romantic Egoists,* a wonderfully illustrated, coffee table biography of Scott and Zelda Fitzgerald, I let them go with the rest of my library, which I sold in 2011.

The man was a hopeless romantic. He called me one day while I was visiting my brother and his wife in Asheville. Said, "Listen to this," put the phone receiver down by his stereo and left it there all the way through Carmina Burana. Like the literature he shared with me, it was glorious. We were both mind-swerving drunk on it.

I was enormously flattered by his attention, by the obvious fact that he had fallen in love with me. I was 28 and writers were my heroes and he was a writer. Again, I lived in my head, and again, for a young woman my age, and a divorcée, no less, I was unbelievably stupid about men. I had no sexual interest in Ralph Dennis, so I ignored his in me. For a long time, he had the good sense, apparently, not to attempt to pressure me into a sexual relationship. As I say, the seduction he practiced upon me was subtle and patient.

Unless his reticence with me was reluctance. He was a balding man with a beer belly in love with a beautiful young thing nearly half his age. He may simply have dreaded my response to any overt demonstration of sexual desire. So, he bided his time. What he had going for him, and he knew it, was my admiration for his intellect, his self-confidence and skill as a writer.

His Christmas gift to me in 1975 was a solid gold pocket watch with an inscription dated 1906. The watch was slender, as if designed to rest in the palm of a lady's hand. It was exquisite and adored it. But I remember that, as I sat alone by my Christmas tree one night, turning the golden wafer of a timepiece this way and that to reflect the colored lights on the tree, I felt inexpressibly sad. The gift was expensive and fairly radiated Ralph's love for me, and I knew that I did not love him the way he wanted me to and that I should not accept the gift. It was his very declaration of love. I gazed at it ticking softly in the palm of my hand, shimmering.

In hindsight, I realize that, with the gift of the watch, our relationship shifted. Ralph became supplicant.

I think it was a couple of months later that Ralph took me to an expensive restaurant in downtown Atlanta and ordered a large plate of oysters oreganata for each of us. I was embarrassed to have to admit that I could not eat oysters (they looked like phlegm on the half shell to me). Ever the compliant gentleman, he ordered me something else and when we left the restaurant, handed the carry-out box of oysters to a homeless man outside the restaurant.

Why in God's name I felt I had to go shopping that afternoon for a lipstick liner I will never know, but we stepped into a department store and while I was at the cosmetic counter, he disappeared. Back outside on the sidewalk in front of the store, he pulled a jewel box from his pocket and opened it. Inside was the largest, most luscious opal (my birthstone) and diamond ring that has ever sparkled before my eyes. He offered it to me as an engagement ring.

I couldn't take it. Although in my selfish desire for his friendship I had ignored all the signs of his having fallen in love with me, I was neither a cruel nor a dishonest young woman. I was embarrassed, so I hedged at first, saying the ring was much too expensive. He ignored that, urging me to put it on. I must have convinced him that I was not ready to marry again, because he finally went back in the store and returned it. I felt he was trying to force me, as if the extravagance and sheer richness of the gift would prove irresistible, but if he thought so, he did not know me. And although the gesture had discomforted, even irritated me, I have never forgotten the disappointment in his eyes when he closed the box and turned with it back into the store.

He was a sad man. Even in my memories of the fun times, of boozy laughter in smoke-filled bars, I remember him as being quiet, reserved, yet smiling, his eyes amused, and if shaken occasionally with chuckles, I don't remember him participating in our uproarious shouting and laughter. In hindsight, I realize that he was a lonely, middle-aged man watching kids having fun.

Behind the amusement, the sad man waited, watching, defeated. He had been defeated all his life by women who did not want him.

When I was in his apartment, I saw a framed photo of a little boy on a pony. Grinning, I asked if it were a picture of him. He nodded. I think he told me then that he had been orphaned very young. I learned only recently, in reading Ben Jones's, *My Friend Hardman*, that Ralph Dennis had siblings and that their mother had left them in an orphanage when he was six or seven years old. That he remembered watching, through the bars of a closing gate, his mother drive away.

I believe that a child abandoned by his mother will carry within himself always the expectation of rejection, that he will lack the sense of self-worth that is essential to achievement—be his goal winning the love of a woman or winning a Pulitzer. I believe that Ralph Dennis, for all his intellect and education and his skill and confidence as a writer, expected defeat. His very posture was that of a defeated man.

I realize now that as a twenty-something, I intuited his sadness, his hopelessness; I knew that his need for me was emotional; I sensed that he wanted to marry me because he needed to own me. I had the vague idea that, if I married him, I would effectively become the prisoner of a jealous and controlling man.

I lost respect for him. I hotly resisted his attempts to hobble me. To bind me.

He'd call me on the phone, arguing his case. He wrote me long letters. Said that if I didn't want to marry him, I could just live with him.

His need was an irritant. Like a fly touching my cheek, my shoulder, the back of my hand. Finally one day, I sat down at my electric typewriter and furiously typed a letter that stated my feelings in no uncertain terms. I remember the white hot fury with which I typed that day, the soot-black marks of the ink ribbon upon the white typing paper, and I remember a bit of the phone call I received a few days later. He said that my letter had been "hammering letter," that it was "castrating."

We had a heated exchange. I was shocked and contemptuous of his feeling of having been castrated by my refusal to marry him. Asserted (truthfully) that I had no idea what he was talking about, that if he thought a woman's refusal to marry him was castrating, then he had a real problem, and so on and on, back and forth, until he said goodbye and I knew that he would never speak to me again.

And but for one short and final sentence, he never did.

A year or so later, I was in Atlanta again visiting the woman who had been one of the gang in the drunken glory days at George's. I took a notion to go to George's, hoping I'd catch Ralph there and that we could, I don't know, hug like old friends again. Something like that. Who knows what the hell I wanted. Just to see him, say hey, be friends again.

I could have had no idea how deeply my rejection had cut him.

Sure enough, he was at the bar talking with another man when we came in. We took our seats at a booth. He gave no sign that he had seen us. I was fairly bouncing with excitement, so happy to see him again.

Finally, he walked over to the table. I looked up with an eager grin, and he said, "I said goodbye to you a year ago, lady."

The coldness of his eyes stunned me, literally stopped my breath. I don't know whether he turned and went back to the bar or walked out. I don't remember anything after that.

I grew up eventually. Now I understand. Now I know.

And I can tell you this much: Ralph Dennis was not Hardman. Hardman was the man he wished to be.

Cynthia Williams is a professional writer whose work includes creative non-fiction, fiction, narrative history, and copy writing for television. The History Press published her *Hidden History of Fort Myers* in 2017, and in 2019, Random House will publish her children's book, *Me and the Sky*. Cynthia has also recently completed a screenplay for an animated film titled, *Happy*. Cynthia lives on an island off Fort Myers, Florida.

# ABOUT THE AUTHOR

Ralph Dennis isn't a household name...but he should be. He is widely considered among crime writers as a master of the genre, denied the recognition he deserved because his twelve *Hardman* books, which are beloved and highly sought-after collectables now, were poorly packaged in the 1970s by Popular Library as a cheap men's action-adventure paperbacks with numbered titles.

Even so, some top critics saw past the cheesy covers and noticed that he was producing work as good as John D. MacDonald, Raymond Chandler, Chester Himes, Dashiell Hammett, and Ross MacDonald.

The *New York Times* praised the *Hardman* novels for "expert writing, plotting, and an unusual degree of sensitivity. Dennis has mastered the genre and supplied top entertainment." The *Philadelphia Daily News* proclaimed *Hardman* "the best series around, but they've got such terrible covers..."

Unfortunately, Popular Library didn't take the hint and continued to present the series like hack work, dooming the novels to a short shelf-life and obscurity...except among generations of crime writers, like novelist Joe R. Lansdale (the *Hap & Leonard* series) and screenwriter Shane Black (the *Lethal Weapon* movies), who've kept Dennis' legacy alive through word-of-mouth and by acknowledging his influence on their stellar work.

Ralph Dennis wrote three other novels that were published outside of the *Hardman* series but he wasn't able to reach the wide audience, or gain the critical acclaim, that he deserved during his lifetime.

He was born in 1931 in Sumter, South Carolina, and received a masters degree from University of North Carolina, where he later taught film and television writing after serving a stint in the Navy. At the time of his death in 1988, he was working at a bookstore in Atlanta and had a file cabinet full of unpublished novels.

Brash Books will be releasing the entire *Hardman* series, his three other published novels, and his long-lost manuscripts.

www.ingramcontent.com/pod-product-compliance
Lightning Source LLC
Chambersburg PA
CBHW072356020726
47506CB00004B/1140